SONIC 2

THE HEDGEHOG

THE OFFICIAL MOVIE NOVELIZATION

PENGUIN YOUNG READERS LICENSES
An imprint of Penguin Random House LLC, New York

First published in the United States of America by Penguin Young Readers Licenses,
an imprint of Penguin Random House LLC, New York, 2022

Visit us online at penguinrandomhouse.com.

Printed in the United States of America

ISBN 9780593387368   10 9 8 7 6 5 4 3 2   COMR

SONIC THE HEDGEHOG 2

THE OFFICIAL MOVIE NOVELIZATION

written by Kiel Phegley

story by Pat Casey & Josh Miller
screenplay by Pat Casey & Josh Miller
and John Whittington

CHAPTER 1

For the first time in his short teenage life, the hyperactive blue hedgehog didn't have to hide. He could run through the streets of Green Hills in broad daylight, unafraid of the townspeople. He made new friends every day. It felt like nothing could slow him down.

So why not make a late-night run out of town by the speed of his own two feet? Seattle sounded nice this time of year. And listening to the police radio's frequencies like Donut

Lord had taught him . . . well, it was just the perfect soundtrack for a one-hedgehog road trip.

That's how Sonic found himself weaving in and out of a high-speed police chase after a stolen armored truck. His signature red sneakers left a track of flames on the ground. The bright blue shine of his quills got an electric super charge. And he even found time to pick up a chili dog off a street vendor!

"We've got company!" cried the getaway driver, sticking his head out the window.

"This oughta slow 'em down!" hollered his partner in the passenger seat, while pulling out a duffel bag of homemade bombs.

"Aw, come on, guys. It ain't the Fourth of July yet. Why not pull over before someone gets hurt?" Sonic called through the window.

"Gah!" the second robber screamed as he

took in the blue blur zipping around at top speed. He immediately lit a bomb and threw it at Sonic.

Pow! The bomb exploded on the street, turning over a mailbox, which the hedgehog easily dodged. This was getting ridiculous. It was time for action and quick.

With a breathtaking turn of speed, Sonic swung into the driver's open window and pushed the crooks across the cab with a few quick kicks to their faces. "Mind if I drive?" he said, gripping the wheel and trying to reach the brake pedal with his dangling feet.

"Mmmpphhbbbmmmbb!" called a muffled voice from the window over Sonic's shoulder. It was a security guard, hog-tied among the money bags in the back.

"I'm sorry, I can't understand you!" Sonic shouted. "Your mouth is covered in duct tape!

But fear not, citizen! I'm the hero you need—*and* the hero you deserve! I am the blue dawn that banishes the darkest night. I am . . . holy crap!" Sonic was about to hit a little old lady crossing the street with a walker is what he was.

SCREEEEEEEEECH! The hedgehog pulled the wheel hard to the right, and the armored truck tipped up on two wheels as the police sirens screamed louder behind them. But the lady made it to the other side!

"Don't worry! Nobody's gonna get hurt!" Sonic called, almost believing it himself. Next to him, the two robbers were knocked out cold, but their bag of bombs slid freely across the front seat! He smiled weakly to the guard in back. "I admit this looks bad, but the bombs aren't lit. So I say again: Nobody's gonna get—" One freshly lit explosive popped loose in the bag, and in a moment, its wick had sparked off another . . . and another! In seconds the entire bag was sparking and smoking with over a dozen fuses burning down to doomsday. "All bets are off! No promises, guarantees, or refunds!"

This was bad, but Sonic had seen worse.

Just eight months back, the hedgehog alien was on the brink of death—battling a mustached madman called Dr. Robotnik. That drone-building maniac had nearly torn Sonic's life apart. But thanks to the help of his best bud, Tom Wachowski (aka the sheriff of Green Hills, Montana, aka Donut Lord), Sonic was able to body-slam Robotnik through an interdimensional portal and off planet Earth forever.

And in that moment, Sonic had touched a kind of action he never thought imaginable.

He had been a hero. And with all that power, he had some kind of responsibility, right? At least the responsibility to kick some bad-guy butt every once in a while.

So this time the bad guys had bashed back with a bag of rapidly burning bombs. So what? Sonic could totally defuse this whole situation before the Seattle PD pushed him off the road and into a fiery ball of death, right?

Swak! A hard hit to his face brought Sonic back to reality. One of the robbers had come to and was furiously trying to knock the hedgehog back out the window. Didn't this clown realize the bombs were set to blow?

"Do you mind? I'm kind of dealing with something here!" Sonic called, and turned the entire duffel bag of bombs over on the criminal's head, knocking him out again. As an insane number of lit bombs fell out, Sonic chucked them out of the truck and into an open dumpster across the street.

Swik-swik-swik-swik-swik . . . KA-BOOOOOM! He tossed the final explosives out just in time to see their new home explode in a stinky fireball. "I've heard of dumpster fires before, but this has got to be a record," Sonic said. "Please hold your applause!"

"Msh-MRRRRRRPH!" the security guard screamed through his taped mouth, and so Sonic ripped off the gag while keeping the other hand on the steering wheel. "There's one bomb left!" the guard shouted. "It's in your spiky things!"

Sonic ran a hand through his quills, which he now noticed were smoking. "Ugh. I can never find *anything* in here!" He grabbed the bomb as the fuse burned down to nothing and threw it at the first sewer grate he spotted.

BOOM! "Drained it from downtown!" Sonic pumped his fist in the air. "See, I told you nobody would get hurt!"

"You're out of control!" called the guard from the back.

"Well, you're not really winning Security Guard of the Year for your performance today, are you?"

Sonic didn't know what the guard was talking about. He totally had this under control! So much so that he absolutely did *not* freak out when he realized he was driving a stolen bank vault on wheels into an ice-cream truck surrounded by kids. "Don't panic!" he yelled. "This is only a drill . . ."

It's a funny thing about speeding along in your life. The faster a superspeedy alien hedgehog could move, the more it seemed like everything went in slow motion. So when Sonic jumped from the truck and pulled off its wheels while it was still in motion, the action felt like a month for him. But the people on the street couldn't see anything more than a hypnotic blue blur, circling around the truck over and over. In a breathless whirlwind of a moment, the armored auto collapsed onto the street—grinding to a halt just inches from the ice-cream truck.

See? Totally under control.

The police cars finally caught up, and the look on their confused faces was priceless. They had a half-dismantled getaway vehicle, a pair of unconscious robbers, and one jittery security guard yammering on about a blue devil. From a rooftop perch, Sonic took it all in and smiled.

"No need to thank me, citizens!" he said, more so to himself than to them. "All in a night's work for . . . Blue Justice!"

As he turned on a heel and headed for home, Sonic felt like life on planet Earth had finally caught up to his speed. He was a superhero now. And there wasn't one force in the entire universe that could slow his rise to the top.

CHAPTER 2

Robotnik rose the same way he had every day for eight months. He felt the same arid, itchy climate. He smelled the same moldy, tangy air. He saw the same mushrooms, mushrooms, mushrooms, mushrooms. Always mushrooms!

His most basic mushroom machine started off the day, raising the shutters of his rotted mushroom palace and letting the eerie red light of this world's sun once again assault his eyeballs. He'd been up all night again. There was no escape from this fungi-infested place but into his own mind.

"X squared times the hypotenuse of Y squared, divided by the absolute value of Z to the third power . . . ," Robotnik mumbled as the room filled with warm light. His eyes were bloodshot and unblinking. "Equals ZY squared!"

"See, Agent Stone?" He whipped around and taunted the rock—his only companion. "Told ya I could solve cold fusion in my sleep! Now rise and shine! Another dawn breaks on our celestial purgatory."

He engaged his morning routine: waxing his magnificent mustache until it was at its twirliest, slathering some makeshift sunscreen on his egg-like dome of a head, and dining on a variety of fungi foodstuffs. To date, his best innovations were the varieties of mushroom stews or grilled 'shroom burgers on extra-shroomy buns that he could cook up. Revolting? Yes. But they fueled his desire for REVENGE! That cold dish that tasted . . . quite a bit like mushrooms.

But all was not lost. No. Robotnik held tight to one idea. He may be living on a fungi-coated spheroid orbiting around a red dwarf star, but he was undoubtably, undeniably, unquestionably the smartest living thing on this planet. Just as he had been on Earth. And how would he keep sharp in the face of endless isolation? By playing the game of true intellects against the only intellect worthy of Robotnik . . . Robotnik himself!

"Shiitake to D4 . . . the Albin countergambit . . . ," he narrated as he spun around both sides of his makeshift mushroom chessboard. "Honey fungus to E7 . . . Lasker's queen sacrifice . . . Agaricus bisporus to G2 . . . Karpov's endgame! Ha . . . suck on that, Eggman!"

Ugh. There was that name again. It had slipped out of his own mouth this time. Eggman. One of the haunting taunts of that vile blue Sonic the Hedgehog. And it burned him up to no end that his only source of power on this planet was the seemingly endless supply of electricity that flowed from the blue quill Robotnik had plucked from Sonic's hide.

Revving up the makeshift dune buggy that was all that remained of his once glorious egg-pod assault vehicle, Robotnik went out for his daily mushroom harvest. Tearing up the landscape brought him some small amount of joy, but today of all days, his path of destruction paid out in unexpected results. After turning over one of the endless variety of toadstools, he saw something he'd never seen before. It was a fungus, for sure, but this one sparkled with a strange purple glow.

In all his months alone, Robotnik had devoured every kind of mushroom on this planet. Broad-capped. Soggy. Mealy. Mushy. Even man-sized. He'd catalogued them all as he went. Another task to keep his mental acuity sharp. Yet this new, shimmering morsel had been hidden beneath the dewiest cap available. Grown in the dankest corner of this funky planetoid.

Robotnik leaned in and plucked the small cap, noting its features. "Color? Byzantium. Bioluminescence? Exceptional. Edibility . . . ?"

He popped it into his mouth. And with

one swallow, the world melted away as his stomach turned itself inside out.

"Agent Stone!" he choked as he fell to the ground. "I don't feel so good!"

"Then maybe you should lie down, sir . . . ," said Agent Stone.

Wait. Did he actually say that? This Agent Stone had always been a voice in Robotnik's exceptionally crowded head. But now he could actually hear it! He saw the stone flap its lips. It had lips! Suddenly, everything went fuzzy.

He was losing control. NO! He never lost control. He was a machine. A perfect, punctual, precise body of scientific conquest. Robotnik refused to let this miniature mushroom topple his flawlessly focused brainwaves. But the world was melting around him now. He couldn't quite make sense of it. Such a reaction would terrify a lesser mind.

Then, suddenly, in that haze of mushroom poisoning, his brain kicked into overdrive. The darkening of his vision became a chalkboard, and Robotnik furiously wrote the equation of his life.

"Speed of light squared," he mumbled as his body writhed on the ground. "The star configurations point past the Kuiper belt . . . and lead our gaze beyond the Milky Way and to THE CENTER OF THE UNIVERSE . . . but where to go from there?"

In an instant, a celestial star chart had formed in his line of sight. He knew exactly where he was! But how could he turn this location to his advantage? Like a dream, the answer appeared in front of him. It was like a giant monolith carved into the shape of a word. To reach out into the galaxy and make a complete connection, all he needed was . . . BACON!

"Wait, that's not right. Forgot to carry the two," he said, staring at the vision of the stone word. "I'd like to buy a vowel, Pat!" And an *E* arrived just in time to sear the concept onto his cerebellum.

"BEACON! That's it! My ticket off this portobello prison. An intergalactic beacon with optical frequency multiplier amplified by intensity radiative flux!" he screamed with joy. That would reach past this armpit of a planet to someplace with intelligent life. Not as intelligent as him, of course . . . but intelligent enough to understand the concept of revenge. "Thank you, toxic alien mushroom that almost killed me!"

Work began right away. All he needed was

properly conductive building materials (the remnants of his egg-pod), infrastructure big enough to construct the beacon (a mountain of mushrooms), and a power source that could generate a cosmic amount of energy (the blue quill pilfered from that blasted hedgehog). Finally, he'd constructed the makeshift broadcast tower worthy of his own genius!

"It's time, Stone," he said to his inanimate granite henchman. "If my calculations are correct—and there's no reason to say 'if,' because they always are—this quill is about to power my masterpiece. Now let's light this candle and see who comes knocking."

Robotnik hacked a series of commands into his one remaining control pad and . . . nothing. "Why isn't it working?!" he shouted in rage. "My calculations are never wrong!

I! AM! NEV-ER! WRONG!"

Shwoooooom! The beacon exploded to life in a wave of eerie blue light. The air warped with a hot burst of energy, and Robotnik was blown back. It had worked. The pain of his progress had launched a shockwave of the quill's own unique energy signature into deep space. All Robotnik had to do was wait. In fact, it felt like the right time for a little nap.

But rest didn't last long. Before the burning sun had set, the air shimmered again.

Zam!

The heat of a golden ring that lit up the surface of the planet . . . And as the circular portal appeared, three figures stepped out.

They were human . . . or humanoid at least. They were certainly no species that anyone on Earth had ever seen. But from the way they walked and the weapon-heavy armor they wore, it was clear these cosmic scoundrels were scavengers of the worst sort. They were creeping up on Robotnik's sleeping body, which dreamed as it clutched tightly to the valuable blue quill.

"BOO!" He snarled to life while pulling another of his ingenious mushroom levers. Robotnik's latest machine sprung into action, and like dominoes falling across a board, mushrooms collapsed all around on the would-be scavengers.

One had its legs taken out from underneath it. Another took a hit directly to the face from "Agent Stone." In the end, all that mattered was that they were on the ground, and Robotnik was on his feet.

"I outsmarted them all!" he cried in triumph. "Not to be supercilious, but by the transitive property I am now *The Smartest Life-Form in The Universe!*" Robotnik danced his way toward the still-wavering ring portal and toward freedom. "Farewell, land of funky fungi!"

But an opposing force unlike any other met him on the other side.

With the sound of thunder, a white fist with two bulbous knuckles jutting out flew through the portal, blasting Robotnik right in his solar plexus. He flew through the air and crashed on his back in a pile of mushrooms.

Above him now loomed a kind of creature he had never seen before. Its fur was as red as rage, and its eyes narrowed suspiciously as it reached down and picked up the blue quill that Robotnik had dropped in his fall.

"Where did you get this?" the creature said.

"From a little blue menace on a planet called Earth." Robotnik smiled. "I'd be happy to show you the way."

CHAPTER 3

Tom Wachowski woke to another perfect morning in Green Hills. The dew on the leaves glistened gently outside his window. The smell of fresh coffee burbling in the pot drifted upstairs from the kitchen. And a trail of slightly singed one-hundred-dollar bills drifted in a cross breeze along the upstairs hallway. Wait. That last one was odd.

Tom knew where the bills came from, of course. But *how* they got there was a question that was the difficult subject to broach. Maybe it was worse than Tom thought.

What had Sonic gotten up to this time?

Sneaking down the hallway and toward the hedgehog's room, Tom peeked through a crack in the door. Sonic was on the floor, hunched over his most prized possessions— a satchel that contained a handful of trans-dimensional rings and an ancient map and the feather of his long-lost mom.

"Hope you'd be proud, Longclaw," the kid said to the feather. "I'm still keeping a low profile, but I had to help them. It's a hero's duty."

"Sonic? You up, buddy?" Tom called in. "Get much sleep last night?"

A flurry of wind shook through the room as Tom opened the door, and he saw Sonic now in bed, the covers pulled up to his neck.

The hedgehog yawned. It was an exaggerated, cartoonish yawn. He hadn't gotten great at lying yet, which was nice. "Can you repeat the question?" Sonic asked.

"Maddie's making pancakes . . . just the way you like them . . ."

Keeping up the act, Sonic stumbled out of bed and out the door, following the scent like an old cartoon. "Pancakes . . . so fluffy . . . like buttery pillows . . ."

Tom wasn't sure how to talk about the mystery bills. Whatever was driving Sonic had something to do with Longclaw . . . the warrior owl that raised him and then sent him to this planet for protection. But he had the Wachowski family to protect him now. Did that make Tom the kid's father? And if he was, there had to be a way to talk to him other than just wagging a finger at the kid for sneaking out. Every time he tried to talk to him about it, Sonic would make something up to distract them, like create a romantic Italian restaurant setting for him and his wife. The candles were a nice touch, but he could've at least brought them some spaghetti.

Maddie, Tom's wife, said that Sonic was a teenager. The last thing they wanted to do was talk about their problems. But Tom couldn't let Sonic just run off and play the blue blur vigilante!

Actually, now that he thought about it, there was one way to get through to him . . .

>>>>>>>

It was an age-old Wachowski family

form of male bonding: fishing. Tom had done it with his dad—even though they never caught anything. But the boat was a place to slow things down and focus on what was important. Plus, once Sonic was out on the water, he was a captive audience. The little guy still wouldn't learn to swim.

"Any bites yet, Sonic?" Tom said after they'd been out on the water fifteen minutes. His shipmate was silent. "Yeah, me neither. Just be patient. It's like my dad always told me: The key to fishing is patie—"

Snoooooooorrrrrrreee! Sonic's nose snorted hard as he fell into a deep sleep on the other side of the boat. His heavy head tilted to one side, then the other, and then it led his whole body off the edge and into the water.

"Gah! Help!" Sonic cried as his face burst from the water. "I can't swim! Call the coast guard! Call the mermaids! Somebody save me!"

Tom reached into the water with a steady hand and pulled his friend back on board, getting a face full of spray up his nose in the process. "You're all right. Calm down," he said. "At least now you had a chance to catch up on your sleep. Maybe now we can have a talk."

"About what?" Sonic looked worried.

"Where do I start? The lying? The sneaking out? This reckless vigilante act?"

"So *this* was your big plan? Trap me on the high seas and bust me? You know that water is my kryptonite!"

"This wasn't a trap." Tom's voice softened. "Me and Maddie are worried about you. We want to know why you're doing this."

"You wouldn't understand."

"Try me. Come on, I'm here to help."

"Help?!" Sonic was forceful, almost angry. "See, that's why I sneak out at night—because you still think I'm the scared little kid you found in your garage. But I'm not. I've grown up. I can take care of myself." He stood up in the boat, his little fists clenched hard. "I don't need anyone's help!"

"I get it," said Tom. "That's how I felt when I was your age—powerful, invincible . . . but you're still a kid, Sonic. You need to slow down."

"Me? Slow down? You know who you're talking to here, right?"

"I know it's hard, but you're supposed to be a teenager, not a superhero."

"And you're supposed to be my friend . . . not my dad!"

There it was. Tom set his jaw and looked at the kid eye to eye. Maybe Sonic was right.

Maybe he'd been pushing too hard to be a parent when that's not what this kid needed at all.

"Okay. I'm not your dad," Tom said finally. "But me and Maddie care about you more than anyone in the world. We are your family. That means no matter how powerful you are, you don't have to do this alone. Sometimes the strongest thing you can do is ask for help."

"Then can you help me prove to you that I'm not 'still a kid'? Besides, you know, being a secret crime-fighting vigilante."

Tom thought about it. If Sonic was going to prove he was responsible, he needed the chance to do it. "What about the wedding?" he offered finally. "Maddie's sister ties the knot next week. I'm leaving Deputy Wade in charge of the town. How about we leave you in charge of the house for the weekend while we go to Hawaii?"

"Really?!?" Sonic's eyes hadn't lit up like that for a month.

"We can try it, *if* you promise to go easy on the junk food, be in bed by nine, not watch any R-rated movies, and—most important of all—STAY HOME."

"Deal! Now let's tell Maddie and make this official!" the hedgehog shouted, and began to paddle the boat so furiously it turned in circles on the water.

"Whoa! Sonic! Remember what I said about slowing down!"

CHAPTER 4

Far above town, a storm was brewing. The cliffs darkened as the wind twisted and turned, picking up leaves and branches in its power as it howled over the hills. The debris swirled in a small twister, and sparks began to flicker in the air as if by magic.

Something big was coming. Something that no one in this world would ever expect.

Zam!

A flash of lightning split a golden ring

in the air, and soft feet landed on the ground.

"If these readings are accurate, he's here," said Miles "Tails" Prower. "I just hope I'm not too late."

The fox adjusted the dials on his handheld tracking device. The computerized scope had guided him for many months and across many worlds. He'd calibrated it perfectly to lock in on the unique chaos energy that radiated from the universe's greatest hero. Well . . . almost perfectly. Tails had reached as many natural disasters, dangerous adversaries, and booby traps as a creature could find in the various zones of galactic civilization on his way. But whenever a planet would prove a dead end, his device would pick up another hint of that power, which seemed to be concentrated in one animal above all others.

"Sonic," he said softly. "What kind of planet did you end up on?"

Splitting his twin tails apart, the fox began spinning them like the blades of an airship and floated up above the green hills of a tiny village on the universe's most backwater planet: Earth. Even the most detailed galactic encyclopedias warned about this place—a land of war-making, animal-trapping primates and their barbaric tech.

Of course, people had been wrong about these things before. They were wrong about Tails, sure enough. He was an inventor, a puzzle-solver, and a go-getter. But when anyone on his home planet looked at him, all they ever saw was what made him different— never what he could do to bring creatures together.

But that could change here. If he could

find Sonic before their enemies did, they might have a chance of saving the universe once and for all. Together. But of course, finding the hedgehog was only step one, and if his readings were correct, there was something much more powerful yet uncovered on this planet.

Tails landed softly on the edge of town and adjusted his tool belt. On that belt, he held everything he needed to survive this or any world: electro-nets, ultrasonic blasters, goo bombs . . . but no more warp rings. This planet was his last jump—his last chance at finding Sonic.

Skulking in the foliage on the side of the road, Tails checked his device again. "He's close. I just need a way to reach him without being spotted," he said, and grabbed a pair of long branches still covered in leaves. Using them as cover, Tails hopped and skipped his way along the road and into town. It was . . . nicer than he expected. The air was sweet. The climate was temperate. But what about these "people"? Were they dangerous?

Just then, one of them walked across the street from Tails' location. He simulated what he assumed was a very convincing bush form, and from beneath his stolen branches, listened to the Earth man's bizarre song.

"Sheriff for the weekend! Sheriff for the weekend! Wade, you are the greatest sheriff for the weekend!" rang out the man's cracking, pitchy voice.

Tails observed the man cross toward a black-and-white transport of some sort. Its engine was already running, and the vehicle looked official with its golden badge on the door. But the man seemed less so.

"Oh, gosh!" the human said, patting his pockets all over. "Where'd my ticket book go? Can't keep the peace without the paperwork, Wade!" He got down on all fours and began to look for the missing manual.

"I get it now," Tails whispered to himself. "They put the village idiot in charge of security."

But the vehicle seemed ideal to aid in Tails' quest. And coming from one officer of the law to a hero-in-training like Tails? Well, it was practically like he was commandeering the car. Borrowing it, really.

"Combustion engine." He marveled at the transport's sputtering motor. "Crude technology, but I can make it work." Tails flew through the open window and studied the gearshift.

"Oh, there you are, you little rascal!" the

man called from the street. "How'd you fall into a sewer grate, huh?"

Tails had only seconds, but there was one key design flaw with the vehicle. A fox of his size couldn't reach the pedals! Tails flipped through the many devices on his tool belt until he found what he needed: his custom-made magne-flops. He slipped the flats over his sneakers, and their bottoms created the barest magnetic effect. They pressed the pedals down without Tails having to touch them.

Vrrroooom!

The transport tore off into Green Hills, and Tails heard the voice of its previous driver cry, "Hey! My car!" He'd have to make it up to him somehow. For one, he was going to have to upgrade this vehicle's capabilities before he brought it back. He could make the changes on the fly, and he'd need to soon if he was going to find Sonic . . . before it was too late.

CHAPTER 5

Sonic had to keep his cool. Even if he was practically bouncing off the walls for a weekend to himself, he couldn't let it show too much. He didn't want to make Donut Lord and Maddie worry. So rather than bounce off the walls, he threw himself into work. And today's work was running Sonic Air.

In truth, there was no airplane involved in Tom and Maddie's trip. Really, the only air they'd travel through was the oxygen floating in the center of the warp ring. But to class it up, Sonic sped his way into the outfit of an airline gate agent. He greeted them as they prepared to step through a ring and into Hawaii.

"Welcome to Sonic Air . . . the fastest way to travel," he said, checking the names on a clipboard. "We will now begin boarding groups one and two."

"Aw . . . Sonic, this is so fun," said Maddie, kneeling down to pat the quills on his head.

"I'm sorry, ma'am. You're in group three. Please wait your turn."

"Woof!" barked the family dog, Ozzy, enlisted by Sonic as airline security.

"Please don't pet the dog, sir. He's working," Sonic said to Tom. His expression remained flat and in character—even if he was a little nervous inside. "Okay, you're free to go now. Buh-bye."

"Not so fast, Sonic. First you gotta bring it in," Tom said, opening his arms wide for a hug.

"Tom, I'm about to be Hedgehog of the House for the first time. I think I'm a little too mature to hug you goodbye."

"How about a power bump?" Maddie compromised. Sonic threw a fist into the air, and when it was joined by theirs, he knew he'd be okay. They'd come back. He wouldn't be left alone again. So he tossed a ring into the air.

"We'll call to check in as soon as we—" Tom started, but . . .

Zam!

The warp closed, leaving Sonic and Ozzy alone in the house. At last. "It's forty-eight hours until they come back." The hedgehog smiled at his animal pal. "We've got six hundred and twenty-eight TV channels, a house full of food, and no supervision. Let's do . . . *everything*."

For tonight, "everything" included jumping on the couch, rolling in piles of junk food, makeover mud masks, skateboarding down the stairs and then stunt-jumping over their wedding crystal. But Sonic couldn't stop there. Total freedom wasn't total freedom if he couldn't run a riding mower through the house. After the joyful shenanigans, he retired to a kiddie pool bubble bath with his favorite pink flamingo floatie (never too careful about drowning) and blasted EDM through the expensive speakers.

But he had to cut his R & R short as a

storm brewed. The dark skies and ominous thunder would've spooked even the bravest hero. Sonic decided to go back inside and settle in for a movie. He had his favorite snacks with him, his most comfortable couch blanket, and his satchel by his side with his phone waiting for Tom's call.

The storm bellowed and boomed louder outside until even Sonic had to turn up the volume to push it out. Then all at once . . . *Zam!* A familiar electric cracking pierced the thunder, and the lights throughout the house went out.

"Woo! Blackout!" Sonic cheered to Ozzy. To him, this was merely the perfect opportunity for spooky-story hour. Pulling his blanket overhead and snapping on a flashlight, Sonic settled down for a few blood-curdling campfire tales . . . but the whimpers from Ozzy gave him pause. "Aw, sorry, buddy . . . Everything's okay," he said.

But then it happened.

The TV snapped to life, drowning the room in gray light and loud static. Sonic tried the remote in the still-darkened room, but it had no effect. Ozzy jumped off the couch and ran to hide. And then all around, the lights began to flicker.

"ENNG!" rang a familiar voice from within the glitchy TV. In a blink, the wild-eyed scientist who haunted Sonic's nightmares filled the entire screen. Robotnik was back. But how? "This is a test, only a test, of the emergency broadcast system!" he called in a mocking monotone. "But it's about to get *real* . . ."

The doorbell rang, and Sonic turned his head toward it slowly. As if in a trance. Panic had slowed him to a halt. "You might want to get that . . . ," Robotnik called from the screen. Then as Sonic shook off his nerves and sprinted to the door, the real deal opened the door and walked through in the flesh.

"You didn't miss me?" Dr. Robotnik sneered. He looked different than before— warped and wild.

"Eggman . . ." Sonic shook his head in disbelief. "I don't know how you got back, but you made a big mistake coming here."

"On the contrary. The only mistake was you thinking you'd won. But that was just a prelude. An hors d'oeuvre. An aperitif . . ."

"I get it." Sonic rolled his eyes. The monologuing on this guy!

"Oh, I don't think you do. But you're about to . . . and so will that idiot sheriff! And his wife! And your little dog, too!"

Fed up, Sonic charged at Robotnik. But a split second before he could smash in the villain's face, a gloved fist careened out of the corner of Sonic's eye and sent him flying. *Wham!* Sonic scrambled up from amid the wreckage of the coffee table that broke his fall, and as the room came back into focus, he saw something he never thought he'd see again . . . an echidna.

Years ago, these creatures had taken everything from him when they killed Longclaw. They made Sonic an orphan—left him alone until Tom and Maddie had accepted him. And now a massive echidna was staring him down.

The animal was muscular, a born bruiser. And his thick red fur grew out in braids that may have well been a weapon of their own. But nothing was compared to his fists.

Beneath white gloves, they held huge knuckle spikes. Sonic could still feel them on his cheek.

"What . . . ? Who are you?" the hedgehog asked.

"Where are my manners?" Robotnik butted in. "Sonic, meet Knuckles. He's my new BFFAE—best friend forever . . . and ever." The villain giddily tap-danced around the room.

"Look, Robotnik, I don't care who you've brought to help you. You're never going to get my power." Sonic's fur crackled with energy as he prepared to run straight through the Eggman's face and into the next county. But this other creature . . . this Knuckles had another idea.

"Do I look like I need *your* power?" he growled at Sonic as his fist sparked with a chaotic red energy like Sonic had never seen. This time, the punch wasn't a warning tap, and somehow Sonic couldn't outrun it. *Smash!* The force of the blow sent Sonic through a wall and out into the night.

"Have fun, you two!" Robotnik's voice echoed from the hole Sonic had just blown through the house. And in a moment, Knuckles had landed on top of him.

"Where is it?" the echidna practically barked.

"Where's what?" Sonic was genuinely confused. Robotnik had always wanted *his* power. That force inside of him that gave him his speed. How could he give that up?

"WHERE IS IT???" Knuckles bellowed again, punching the ground so hard its shockwaves sent Sonic flying off the shattering patio.

Sonic looked up with hazy vision and saw what he now knew were his two greatest enemies in the world towering over him.

"So nice when diabolical evil lives up to the hype," Robotnik laughed.

"You talk too much." Knuckles' eyes were fixed on Sonic with rage. "Give it to me!" he demanded once more.

"You asked for it . . ." Sonic breathed deep and charged up for his signature attack. He crouched into running position while this red bully continued to taunt him.

"I was expecting more from you. You're unskilled, untrained . . . and unworthy."

"But I'm not going down without a fight!" Sonic cried, and spun into a sparking spin ball for a full-velocity attack. But Knuckles stopped him dead! He twirled Sonic's body like a basketball. The momentum was sickening. Was this what people meant when they talked about motion sickness? Somehow Knuckles' powers perfectly pushed back on Sonic's own abilities.

Crunch! The echidna body-slammed the hedgehog to the ground and then picked him up by the neck. Sonic struggled as he stared down his adversary, but he wouldn't show any fear. "It is my destiny to do what my ancestors could not—to restore the ultimate power to the home of my people!" Knuckles recited the words like a prophecy.

"Ultimate power, you say?" Robotnik was almost startled at the words. It was Sonic's opening. He had to get them distracted.

"I don't know what you're talking about . . . You've got the wrong guy!" The hedgehog reached his hands toward the rubble. He saw his satchel, blown outside in the shockwave and tangled in a mess of broken furniture.

"Don't play dumb with me." Knuckles shook him hard. "Child of Mobius. Apprentice of Longclaw."

"You knew Longclaw?"

"Longclaw and her people were the sworn enemy of my proud echidna tribe. We fought and died at their hands, and now you will die at mine." Knuckles squeezed Sonic's throat, and the world around Sonic started spinning into darkness.

Wee-oooo! Wee-oooo! Sonic never guessed that the last noise his brain would produce was identical to the Green Hills police car siren, but there it was ringing in his brain. Wait. That wasn't just in his head! The siren was in the air. The squad car crashed through the fence and—*Wham!*—directly over Knuckles' smug bully face.

Sonic struggled to his feet and heard a young voice with a tone of amazement in its words. "Aw, man, I need to recalibrate these brakes. Do you think he's okay?"

Glancing up at the revving car, Sonic beheld a kid just a shade younger than himself. It was a young fox, and it reached out from the car's driver's seat with an open hand. "Get in!" he said. "I'm on your side!" Sonic grabbed his satchel and followed the fox's lead.

CHAPTER 6

Sonic had to think fast. Somehow, Robotnik escaped Mushroom Planet—and he brought a friend with him. It was too wild to think about!

Speaking of friend, Knuckles was surely on their trail by now, but whatever powers the echidna had to block Sonic's speed, he didn't seem to travel so fast himself.

"Wow! Let me just say that it is an honor to finally meet you, Sonic. Is it okay if I call you Sonic?" The fox chattered away as he whipped the squad car through the neighborhood at one hundred miles an hour. "Everyone calls me Tails. You're probably wondering why."

"Because of the extra tail?" Sonic guessed as the furry twin appendages wagged behind Tails.

"That's right! I should have known you'd get it."

"Cool. Very cool," the hedgehog said, and took a deep breath. "Also: WHAT IS GOING ON?! Robotnik is back? And who is Clifford, the big red rage monster?"

"That's Knuckles. He's the most dangerous warrior in the galaxy. He thinks you're the key to finding the Master Emerald." Tails spoke like these were commonly known facts. Like this craziness was no different than knowing what was on TV that night.

"The Master Emerald?" Sonic recalled the term from his childhood; legends that Longclaw would tell him. "That's just a bedtime story."

"No, it's real. It's just been hidden. And its location is the most closely guarded secret in the universe," Tails said. "I should know. I think I'm one of the few left still looking for it."

The fox sped the borrowed cruiser toward the center of town, but it still wasn't as fast as Sonic was. He just needed to clear his head and then he could set out on his own. A hero didn't need to involve anyone else in his danger—not even the only other person who had any idea what was going on.

"I'm picking up an energy signal." Tails checked a handheld device that booped rapidly. "Knuckles must be pursuing us. We've got to make a move!" Ahead, a blinking traffic light turned red.

"Red light! Red light!" Sonic shouted, and pulled the wheel hard. They swerved around the corner just in time to miss oncoming traffic. And in the rearview, Sonic saw Knuckles for a split second. He was galloping along down the street, his fists digging chunks out of the pavement.

"Maybe we can lose him?" the hedgehog mused.

Sha-Boom! The red menace smashed through a water truck behind them, bursting the tranquility of Green Hills and sending townsfolk screaming. "This is ridiculous! I could get out and run faster than this!"

"I'm on it!" Tails grabbed Sonic by a wrist excitedly. "Just don't go anywhere. Promise?

Promise you won't go anywhere?"

"Yes! Yes!" he hurriedly said as Tails ducked under the console of the squad car. "What are you doing under there?"

"Upgrades!" Tails called back. "This law vessel has plenty of capacity for raw power, but it needs to be more properly distributed to all the wheels. Hold on to your quills!" Tails popped up, cranked a gizmo he'd plugged into the motor, then Sonic watched the background recede in a blur. Knuckles was there for a moment but seemed to dive off the street in the wake of their hyperboosted descent.

Sonic slid over and took the wheel. He steered them up the winding paths that led into the mountains and out of town. "Now that we're out of harm's way for a moment, could you explain how you know so much about me?"

"Are you kidding?" Tails was practically hopping up and down on the seat. "Everyone knows about Sonic the Hedgehog! I've spent my whole life learning about you. And when I found out Knuckles was trying to track you down, I came to Earth to help you stop him."

"But why does everyone think I'm the key to finding the Emerald?"

"Because Longclaw was the keeper of the Emerald's secret," Tails explained. "For centuries, her Owl Tribe sought to control the Emerald's Chaos Powers. But eventually, they came to see it as unstable, and they hid it somewhere even their greatest enemies wouldn't look. But you . . . you were supposed to be different. Longclaw's final protégé . . . her greatest discovery. They say you can harness the Emerald's energy like no one before. So it must be here on Earth!"

Sonic stared into the distance, scarcely believing this could be true.

"She didn't tell you about any of this?" Tails asked after an awkward pause.

"No! All I got from her was a bag of rings, her undying love, and an old map."

"A map?" The fox lit up.

WUNK.

Impossibly, Knuckles' fist dug deep into the passenger door, and in one smooth motion, the echidna shredded the door entirely. With eyes that burned like fire, he reached in for Sonic.

"This guy is so obsessed with me!" Sonic cried as he pulled the wheel wildly across the road, shaking their pursuer loose for just a moment.

Tails turned to Sonic as Knuckles' one remaining grip on the doorframe twitched in the corner of his eye. "I've got an idea. Do you trust me?" he asked.

"NO!" the hedgehog replied, but it was too late for protests at this point.

Tails yanked hard on the wheel the other way, shooting the car off the road and toward a thick metal guardrail along the edge of a cliff. It hit with incredible force, and the sound of twisting metal and shattering glass was only barely tamped down by Sonic's screams as the damaged vehicle launched off the cliff.

Knuckles let go at last, digging his fists deep into the rocky cliffside. But there was no way for Sonic to jump out of the the car safely. The ground below began to rush up as they plummeted. The car fell and burst into flames far below.

"AHHHHHH!" Sonic screamed, his eyes shut tight. But when he realized he didn't die, he opened one eye to discover . . . "We're flying?"

Tails' two tails were more than just for looks! He had grabbed Sonic before the car crashed to the ground. The tails spun around like chopper blades, holding both creatures aloft. "Did your butt just turn into a helicopter?" Sonic asked, gobsmacked.

"Ha! Butt-copter! Only Sonic the Hedgehog could come up with something like that!" the kid shouted. "So do you have somewhere safe we can go?"

"Yeah," Sonic said, ready to put them back on path to survival. "I know a place."

CHAPTER 7

Never having stooped to the level of doing manual labor like yard work, Robotnik had assumed the riding mower would move faster than twelve miles per hour. But as he rattled away from the Wachowskis' pitiful abode on that pathetic contraption, his control pad finally reconnected to the planet's web of wireless signals. It was time for Robotnik to get his mojo back.

"If you want something done right, you

gotta hire someone you can push around," the scientist said, and slashed in the code for an invasive, data-sweeping algorithm. Nothing could hide his target from him now. But even Robotnik was surprised to find that the lackey he was looking for was right there in Green Hills . . . at something called the Mean Bean Café.

Robotnik autodialed the number. It took three rings for someone to pick up . . . far too long a lag time.

"Mean Bean," came a voice that Robotnik had been belittling in his dreams for months. "Barista Stone speaking."

"Hey, pencil-neck! Where's my coffee?!" came an agro voice in the background. Probably a slack-jawed stooge like a trucker, knowing this dump of a town.

Robotnik growled one command into the

line and let the natural hierarchy of his world fall into place. "Prepare my latte!" was all it took, and Agent Stone's voice perked up with a new, robot-like urgency. "Sorry, folks. I have to close early."

"I'll leave when I'm ready, twerp," the trucker's voice snapped back. He didn't know what he was in for.

"I didn't want to have to do this . . . ," Stone's icy voice said, and with a loud *chop!* the line was overwhelmed with the screams of would-be interlopers. After a moment, Stone whispered into the line, "The goat's milk is steaming, sir." And then communications cut off.

The next part of Robotnik's plan would require some more finesse. And so—despite his clear superiority—Robotnik did something he would never have dared before. He waited.

Arms akimbo, the doctor turned his head to the sky and counted the minutes. The indignity of this mower ride. The taste of stale mushrooms still on his tongue. In a moment, it would all be washed away with the arrival of his babies.

Bzzzzzzzz!

Yes, there they were in the distance now. Robotnik could hear their perfectly calibrated motors from miles away. His proudest creations. His deadly drones. His beautiful drones! From high in the sky, the red-eyed droids floated down and around him. They'd been set free from their secret satellite housing unit by Stone's preplanned activation protocols. And now they could transform him back into the Robotnik he was made to be.

With a whirl of their jet-black metal bodies, the drones swirled around their master, replacing his tattered clothes with a flowing red flight jacket. They even styled his mustache so it was extra aerodynamic. And finally, several of the drones combined to create a floating throne for Robotnik to travel on in style.

Robotnik guided his new transport toward the burning site where all indicators showed his ally had failed. At the top of the cliff, he could hear the disgruntled strains of the bruising red alien called Knuckles as he clawed his way up the rock face and to the street. This muscle-bound miscreant was dangerous. Dangerous but useful. And Robotnik knew just how to play Knuckles to his advantage . . . the direct approach!

"So, my massively metacarpaled friend . . . you mentioned an ultimate power back at the house?" the scientist asked.

"The Master Emerald? It does not concern you. I got you off that planet of mushrooms, and you brought me to the hedgehog. We have no more use for one another."

"Actually, I think we might . . . Earth is my turf." Robotnik swept his gaze wide across the night sky. "I rule this terrestrial spheroid. I know every element, every phylum, every species that has ever slithered, buzzed, or dabbed on this planet."

"I understand nothing you just said."

"Allow me to explicate, annotate, and elucidate so that you may better postulate. If you remove E and T from 'my planet,' it spells 'my plan.' My planet, my plan! See? I help you retrieve this Emerald, and you use it . . . to destroy the hedgehog."

"You're suggesting an alliance?" Knuckles was finally beginning to grasp the situation . . . or at least as much of it as Robotnik would allow.

"The echidnas do not enter easily into such arrangements." Knuckles beat his chest with bravado. "It requires the removal of our internal organs and the reinsertion of each inside the chest cavity of another."

"Charming, but a tad invasive." Robotnik floated his chair out of reach. "Around here we simply grip each other's hands tightly."

"That's it? It seems very simplistic."

"Well, I've always believed that less is more . . . AHHH!" The miscreant had crushed Robotnik's own knuckles in its meaty white paw. "Ow! Ow! Ow! You truculent space bumpkin! You crushed my favorite hand!"

"Really? My hand is uninjured," Knuckles said with a shrug. "But I am now convinced of your commitment."

"Next time we swap organs!" Robotnik's ego was bruised, but he had to keep his cool. Staying one step ahead was his only option to keep his plan in motion.

With the hedgehog having flown the coop, Robotnik determined their best bet was to build up capabilities at the Mean Bean. The place was a disgusting picture of traditional hometown values, but the doctor had faith there was more under the surface.

"You said you could find the hedgehog. Why are we wasting time at a common eatery?" Knuckles complained as they entered.

"Have faith, my contemptible compadre. If my hypothesis is correct, this wake-up joint is more like a sleeper cell . . ." And at that hint, Agent Stone stepped out from the back room, a look of giddy excitement on his face.

"Doctor! It's really you!" he cried. "You look different . . ."

Robotnik brushed the tips of his sunburned mustache and considered his frame in his window reflection. He looked more roguish than he ever thought possible. "Papa's got a brand new 'stache!" he beamed.

"And you've brought . . . some kind of space porcupine?"

"I am an echidna warrior, trained since birth in all forms of lethal combat, destined to restore honor to my tribe, and willing to destroy anything that gets in my way." The echidna reached out and crushed Stone's hand without blinking an eye. Robotnik's underling fell to his knees in pain. An appropriate position, considering his place in the hierarchy.

"That means he trusts you, Stone," the

doctor said. "Now let's renovate this dump!"

Stone stepped up to the chromium pipes of the café's high-end coffee maker, placing his face in front of the main steamer where a red electric sensor was suddenly activated. The light of the retinal scan blinked up and down his eye, and in a moment, the tanks and fixtures of the machine began to shift and rotate, transforming into something completely new.

"I followed your instructions to a tee, sir," Stone said as a computer screen emerged from inside the bean grinder. "From *The Robotnik Manifesto*, section five, article twelve: 'In the event of my capture, disappearance, or account suspension on social media, construct a secure safe house built to my exact specifications and await my return.'"

He'd memorized it. A nice touch, but Robotnik was more impressed that the mobile command center that had just assembled itself in the coffee shop contained his sound system and treadmill. Even a genius needs to get his steps in.

"Sir, there is something you should know," Stone said in a sheepish tone.

"Is there? Bring it."

"After you vanished, the government dissolved all record of your identity."

"What?!?" Robotnik was used to seething with anger at the rubes in Washington, but this was beyond the beyond. "Those mouth-breathing Penta-goons! They think they can make me disappear?!"

"They also froze our assets and bank accounts," Stone said.

"That's nothing a little 'high tex-ploitation'

can't solve!" Robotnik quickly hacked his way through a few dozen billionaires' bank accounts for funds while Stone brought him a fresh latte. "They'll never get away with it, sir," he said.

"One step at a time, Stone." Robotnik grinned, finally fully in his element. "A proper revenge on this planet and its feeble protectors requires direction, dedication . . . and one dead hedgehog."

CHAPTER 8

In his brief time on planet Earth, Tails had
made a few critical observations. The animals
in this world tended to walk on all fours. The
humans left lights on all night in a stunning
waste of energy. And for some reason, even
people with a lot of friends needed space to
be alone. That last one was the hardest idea to
parse.

But that's just the kind of place Sonic
had led him: a secret enclave. A world away

from the world. Something he called "Wade's garage."

As they floated down toward the cube-shaped building and its retractable door, Tails nervously spotted its owner—the town's deputy sheriff. Wade was on his hands and knees again, trying to thread a chain through the gears of a bicycle.

"Steal my car if they will, but that won't keep this cop off the streets," the man mumbled to himself. "As soon as this bike is greased up . . . look out, jaywalkers!!"

"I've encountered this man before," Tails whispered as they walked up to the garage door. "He does not seem familiar with basic mechanical operation."

"Who, Wade?" Sonic said. "Don't underestimate him."

"OW! That pinches!" Wade cried as his

fingers got caught up in the bike chain.

"Don't overestimate him, either," Sonic said, and led the fox into the dimly lit workshop. "Hey, Wade! You all right over there?"

"Hey, Sonic. Everything's great, man. Just fixing up the old bika-roony," the man said, spinning a wheel. "Thought I might get myself back in shape. Plus, someone maybe kind of stole the squad car."

Tails hid behind his hero. Sonic seemed to treat the native humans so kindly. It was clear the fox was going to need a new approach to repair his connection to this world.

"So, Wade . . . I want you to meet Tails. He's not from around here, like me."

"Is your headquarters secure?" Tails immediately began scanning the workshop with his devices. If he could prepare the garage for a siege battle, it might make up for the car.

"This place? Super secure," said Wade. "Nobody gets in or out—except my mom. And the worst thing she'll do is try to make us a snack plate. Welcome to the Wade Cave . . . which is something I hope I can say to a girlfriend someday."

Tails took the map out of Sonic's satchel and spread it across a makeshift table in the center of the room. In the light, the fox could see its stated purpose: pictures of worlds within worlds. Every habitable planet on this side of the universe was represented by visual markers. Looking at these would allow anyone who bore warp rings to teleport across the stars. It could have helped Tails when he was searching for Sonic, but tech had always been the fox's strong suit. And he knew he could put that to good use now.

"I always just thought this was a map of places I could hide . . . and other weird things I didn't understand at all," Sonic said.

"It's more than that." Tails leaned in close to examine some shimmering ancient writing along the map's edge. "Watch this. Hold it up to the moonlight." Tails and Sonic lifted the map up to the window, and as the beams of moonlight shone through, they amplified the writing. It was as if they were charging ancient electrical circuits embedded in the paper. And the circuits in turn projected the shape of a familiar owl into the air above their heads.

"Longclaw . . . ," Sonic said in an awed tone.

"Hello, Sonic," the wise owl began. "If

you're watching this, then something has happened to me. I'd hoped to tell you this story when you were older, but it appears fate has chosen a different path . . . Ages ago, a fearsome group of warriors known as the echidnas gathered the seven Chaos Emeralds, gems of extraordinary power. In their quest for strength, they combined them with the Master Emerald, creating the most unstoppable weapon ever created.

"With this power, a single warrior could defeat entire armies. It amplifies what's in your heart, good or evil. It turns thoughts into reality.

"Believing no one should have that power, my ancestors stole the Emerald and hid it. The secret of its location was passed down generation to generation, hero to hero. I am all that remains of my order. All except for you, my good-hearted little Sonic. Use this map. Find the Master Emerald and protect it. I'm sorry I couldn't be there for you, Sonic."

Longclaw's image faded away, and the trio stood in awed silence.

"Can you play that again?" Wade said at last. "I got, like, none of that."

"She means that the Master Emerald is the ultimate concentration of power in the known universe," Tails explained. "And only Sonic has the power to track it, contain it, and keep it away from Knuckles and this Robotnik. All we've got to do is follow these directions." Tails tapped the map with a small tool, sending a current through its advanced circuitry. The parchment transformed before them into a new kind of map . . . a map full of mountains, oceans, and more recognizable elements.

"Whoa," said Wade, for once echoing what they were all feeling. "Is this where you guys come from?"

"No," Sonic said. "This is Earth."

"Looks like the first clue is hidden in these mountains in eastern Siberia." Tails quickly compared the diagram to a chart on his tracker device. "There we'll find a compass that will guide us to the location of the Emerald."

Sonic crossed his arms. "There's still so much I don't understand," he said. "Knuckles mentioned something about . . . Mobius?"

"The traditional home of our kind," Tails said. "If Knuckles gets his hands on the Emerald, it's not just this world that will be in trouble, Sonic. They say the Master Emerald grants its bearer power to bring anything they think into reality. But it's too chaotic. That's why Longclaw's tribe hid it. No one can hold that power and remain uncorrupted."

"If Knuckles gets the Emerald, he'll finish what his ancestors started and conquer the entire universe," Sonic said. "Too bad for him he can't catch me in a million years."

Seeing his hero boast like that made Tails beam. He knew he'd made the right choice to come. "Now all we have to do is get to the compass before Knuckles can attack."

"I knew a Knuckles in middle school," Wade said, trying to be involved. "He could put his whole fist in his mouth. If this is the same guy, we are screwed."

"Not the same guy—though your Knuckles also sounds bad. But ours is worse," Sonic said. "And he's got an evil supergenius helping him. We have to get the Emerald before they do. And we have to keep this a secret. Understand that, Wade? I won't put Tom and

Maddie in harm's way. That's not what heroes do. I gotta go at this alone."

"Maybe you could use a handy fox?" Tails asked, and when Sonic nodded, the fox was filled with an electric feeling all his own. Their adventure was just beginning, and Sonic promised his number one fan, "I'll find a way for both of us to get there."

CHAPTER 9

Sonic had been all around the world. He'd rolled down the great pyramids of Egypt. He'd done loop-the-loops along the curves of the Golden Gate Bridge. He'd even shredded a few sick snowboard tricks in the powder on the mountains near home. But Siberia? A land of perpetual ice and no chili dogs for thousands of miles was *not* his idea of a hot vacation spot.

And sure, he and Tails were able to

pinpoint a general area in the Russian wasteland that corresponded with the clue on their new map, but the ring he activated from his satchel still dumped them in the middle of nowhere. They were likely miles off the mark in one of the worst blizzards Sonic had ever seen.

"I absolutely cannot find my way! We'll never get there!" Sonic moaned. At least they had bundled up with a pair of oversize overcoats and hats that protected their bodies *and* their identities. But warm clothing couldn't cover up one concrete fact. "We are completely, totally, unequivocally lost!"

Tails slapped a hand on the side of his chaos tracker device. "In this weather, there's no way we're gonna get readings on this thing. Should we go back?"

"No. There's a light up ahead. Maybe we

can take shelter in there!" In the distance, Sonic could make out a tavern in the snow. It was a broken shack of a bar. The kind of place you'd never take a date. The kind of place that Sonic naturally meshed with.

As they approached, the hedgehog wove his way through dogsleds. "Listen, I've been in a place like this before, and things get rough *very* quickly. Just follow my lead and we'll be okay. Got it?"

"Got it," said Tails.

They stepped into the dim light of the bar and kept their heads low. They were already the shortest creatures in the place. Sonic couldn't risk their real forms freaking out the locals . . . especially locals like these. A quartet of gamblers crowded a green-topped table— one of them with a wicked scar across his face. Even the bartender had an eye patch. And in the corner, the world's most unsettling granny knitted a shawl showing an ax splitting a skull.

"Thanks, we'll try the next nightmare barn . . . ," Tails said, and turned to go out.

"C'mon, Tails." Sonic pulled his partner back. "We're going in. Just be careful that we don't end up as the blue plate special."

A scowling waitress dropped two brown paper menus on their laps and asked something in Russian. Sonic didn't understand the words, but the tone felt somewhere in between "What do you want?" and "How should I hurt you?" The hedgehog quickly called up all the Russian words he knew.

"Uh, we'll take two borschts on rye, please!" he stammered.

Quirrp?

Tails produced another of his gizmos; this one had a little spinning speaker at its center. "Two beef stews, please," the little fox said into the device, and in short order, a flat voice translated the order into Russian. The waitress seemed satisfied at least and went off toward the kitchen.

"Man, where'd you get all these cool gadgets?" Sonic asked.

"I invented them." Tails shrugged sheepishly. "It's kind of my thing."

"Pretty impressive."

With a cold clatter, two bowls of gray slop landed on the table before them. The waitress stood with hands on hips, staring the two down with disgust. Tails picked up a bare set of fish bones from within his soup. "I'm sorry, but I asked for the beef stew."

Quirrp! Queep!

.

His little device ran the comment through and spat out some more Russian. This time, it did not seem to do the trick. In fact, the waitress was highly offended by whatever the machine translated. Sonic couldn't tell what she was talking about, but his best guess was, "How dare you insult my beloved grandmother!"

"There must be some confusion. I just mean that this isn't what I ordered!" Tails said in a nervous hurry. With another *Quoorp!* the machine recited more Russian, and now half the bar was looking at them with angry eyes.

"Dude, what is going on?" Sonic asked.

"I don't know!" Tails fiddled quickly with the device as the men at the poker table rose up and shouted what must have been something like, "Who said our mothers were three-legged goats?!"

Sonic stepped in their way, a cool smile on his face. "Okay, take it easy!" he said, hands up. "I'm sure there's a perfectly good explanation for whatever my friend said or did."

Quip-pip-puuurrrp! The gizmo sputtered out like a fart, and with a last few lines of broken Russian from its speaker, the locals went wild. They tore at Tails' and Sonic's coats, exposing the two creatures for the very much nonhumans that they were.

"C'mon, guys! Why does this kind of misunderstanding always happen to me?" Sonic laughed as the crowd of ruffians pushed them into a corner.

Tails flipped through the screen of another device pulled from his bag of tricks and shouted, "Pivonka! Pivonka!"

The crowd stopped. In a snap, their faces went from rage to bemused wonderment.

"Uh, Tails? What does 'Pivonka' mean?" Sonic nervously called over his shoulder.

"I just looked up 'Siberian conflict resolution' in my intergalactic glossary, and . . . uh-oh." Tails' face went slack. "As a custom for solving disputes, it's . . . it's a dance battle."

From behind the mob of humans, a towering figure emerged. He wore a shimmering track suit that barely stretched over mountains of muscle. As he smiled, a gold tooth glittered, and he said, "Da . . . Pivonka!" The crowd erupted into cheers at the arrival of their apparent dance champion.

"Tails, what did you just get us into?" Sonic asked as the floor was cleared of tables to form a makeshift battleground.

"This says if we win, they let us go. But if we lose, it's into the fire."

"We have to grab the map and get out of here." Sonic dug through his satchel and came up short. "But where is the map?!"

"I left it on the table—oh no!" Tails was panicking. "What do we do?"

Sonic stretched his legs, furrowed his brow, and felt the groove of the ancient Soviet techno tune pumping out of the jukebox. "We dance," he said. "And then we get the map and get out of here."

The dance battle was fierce. Two of the gamblers from the table spun onto the floor in perfect synchronization as they kicked at each other, mock-slapped each other, and even flipped each other in flawless form.

Sonic and Tails stepped up in response . . .

and tripped over each other's feet.

"BOOOO!" the crowd taunted as the first round clearly slid out of their reach. As the next song changed to a traditional Russian number, another set of dancers arrived, their arms crossed on their chests and their eyes intense beams of hatred.

"Follow my lead!" Sonic called, guessing where this was going. He crouched low and started busting out his own set of squat kicks with Tails struggling to keep pace. The Russians got lower and lower, kicking out their boots in perfect unison, getting closer and closer to Sonic and Tails until they collided! Boots flew fast, smacking bystanders in the face. At best, the round was a draw, but the audience was as bloodthirsty as ever.

In the excitement, Sonic saw the map

fluttering at the edge of their table across the room. "The map!" he called. "Let's grab it!"

But as they dove for the prize, another of the burly bar regulars snapped it up and held it high. "You want this?" he taunted. "Come get it . . . you freaks!" The crowd started to chant, "Freaks! Freaks! Freaks!" And Sonic could tell that the taunts touched a part of Tails that was deep in his heart. The fox withered to a miserable state.

"Come on, Tails! I need you here!" Sonic called.

"I can't do it, Sonic! I'm not brave like you. My gadget got us into this mess, and I lost your map . . . and now we're gonna get tossed into the fire!"

Sonic rushed to his new friend's side. "Come on, pal. I've got a plan, but I need your help. You with me?" Tails nodded his head slowly, then Sonic whispered the plan in his ear. Step one in executing his scheme saw Sonic quickly switching the jukebox to some real American dance grooves.

Sonic took to the floor and pushed back the crowd with a wicked spin. And with enough space cleared, he was able to kick up every pop, lock, shuffle, and shake he'd learned from years spent alone binging music videos in a cave. Sonic slid his feet across the floor and went into another spin, twirling faster and faster until the crowd grew dizzy watching his hyperfast moves. His quills even started to electrify as he turned into a pure tornado of dance.

And then it was time for Tails' part. After recording Sonic's sweet routine with one of his holographic gadgets, Tails began to project image after image of Sonic rocking out onto every corner of the bar. Before long, there was nowhere a person could look without seeing the spinning hedgehog.

The motion was too much for the Siberians as one by one they fell to the ground. Several dove toward the bathrooms to toss their cookies. By the end of the song, only the map holder still stood, but his knees were weak. As the song reached its crescendo, the hedgehog did a somersault over the heads of his holographic counterparts and landed at the man's feet. With a simple blow from his lips, the exhausted bully finally collapsed. The map was theirs again, and so was the Pivonka!

〉〉〉〉〉〉〉〉

Later on, the fire had burned down to embers. The Russians were either passed out or moved on, and Sonic and Tails lounged in a back corner, relieved to have survived.

"Thanks for having my back, Sonic," the fox said. "Earth seems like a tough place to be on your own."

"Stick with me, pal. I know everything about this ol' pale blue dot."

"Do you really mean that? About me being your pal?"

"Sure, buddy!" Tails wrapped his arms around Sonic in a fierce hug.

"Whoa. Take it easy!"

"Sorry," Tails said, wiping a tear from his eye. "Growing up, I didn't have any friends. Everyone in my village thought my two tails were weird."

"I know that feeling."

"I hated being different. But then I heard about you. The fastest creature in the galaxy. You were weird, too, but you were a legend! It made me think that maybe being weird wasn't so bad. You inspired me, Sonic—inspired me to leave my village and come here to help you in your mission."

Sonic looked at him. He hated to admit it, even to himself, but he didn't think he could have come this far without the little guy's help.

"I'm glad you're here, Tails," he said finally. "But we might as well get some sleep, and this feels as good a place as any to spend the night. Maybe you can get some clear readings on the Emerald once the storm has blown over." And with that, they settled into a restless slumber. Tails' tails stuck out from the blanket and wrapped around Sonic, keeping him warm.

CHAPTER 10

As a noonday sun crested the peaks higher up in the mountains, the snowstorm had finally calmed. They were close. Sonic knew it. He could feel something calling to him down in his quills.

"I pinpointed the coordinates! It's right up ahead!" Tails called, floating in the air above. He held a solid grip on Sonic, his twin tails spinning away. Gliding across the frigid sky, the pair swung toward the face of the mountain, where a deep crevasse was cut into the granite.

As they flew in, the lights of Tails' tracking device began to shine off the walls, and it was clear that this was no ordinary cave. It was a temple. Hidden deep within the rock who knows how many years ago when the Owl Tribe had visited Earth for a time.

When they landed inside the cavern, Tails turned on a portable light. In front of them, ornate carvings of owl warriors battling against spiny-haired figures covered a wall in a massive single scene. It was like a memory pulled from Sonic's nightmares, reliving the day he lost Longclaw forever.

"It says here the owls and echidnas have been fighting each other for centuries," Tails said.

"Like Vin Diesel and the Rock," Sonic

joked, trying to cover up the discomfort he felt.

"And now Knuckles is the last echidna left."

"The last of his kind," Sonic said in a whisper. "So he's been all alone . . ."

They came to the end of the cave, and above them loomed a huge owl statue under a ceiling of sharp stalactites. At the base, Sonic could make out the carved shape of an Emerald in the stone—one with familiar symbols around it. "I've seen these symbols before . . . and I know where!" he realized.

Taking out their map, Sonic traced a finger over the same set of symbols, just in a different configuration. With a trembling hand, he reached out and turned the stone versions like keys to match the map. *Whoom!!* The Emerald carving lit up green along with the eyes of the great owl. The sound of ancient stones grinding together echoed as the owl's chest opened up—ice and dust floating off its wings—and from within the chest floated something else . . . something small.

"A compass!" Sonic cried as the item lowered itself to their level. He snatched up the device, and as the light from the owl faded, the compass began to glow with its own energy, revealing an expansive map of the Earth in a similar projection to the electric letters on the map.

"This will lead us to the Emerald!" Tails realized.

Sonic felt a sense of relief as he looked into the excited eyes of his young companion. But what was that on Tails' head? It looked like . . . a red light!

"Tails, look out!" Sonic yelled, tackling Tails just before the laser sight of Robotnik's drones opened fire on the fox's face.

"RUN!" Sonic commanded, and sprinted off through the cave, nearly a dozen drones flying after them. It was the Eggman's drones. They'd been found!

SHOOOOM!

A miniature missile rocketed over their heads and struck the arch that made the cave's entryway. Their window outside collapsed into a hundred pounds of snow, ice, and rock. They were trapped!

"Yodel-ay-hee-hooooooo!" cried a familiar, blustery voice from above. "Heads up, my little stalagmites!"

In the gloom, Sonic made out the figure of Robotnik bursting through the ice sheets above their heads. He rode in a massive egg-pod with turrets of guns and razor-sharp claws spinning all around its body. "Thanks for all your hard work," the mad scientist cried.

"But *we'll* take it from here!" came the voice of Knuckles from behind Robotnik. The echidna crashed to the ground and swung out massive fists in Sonic's direction, practically clawing after the compass.

"How'd you find us?" Sonic asked.

"You've been walking around with a tracking beacon," Robotnik sneered as he hovered closer. Sonic checked his quills but found nothing. "It's your phone, you furry little dimwit! Consider yourself triangulated, extrapolated, and about to be . . . eliminated."

"You sound pretty smart, but it's hard to take you seriously with those snotcicles in your mustache," Sonic smirked. "Seriously, what kind of genius shows up to Siberia in an open canopy?"

"The kind of genius who can heat things up with the flick of a switch!" replied Robotnik, and with just such a motion, a fiery missile rocketed out of the egg drone directly at Sonic, who redirected the missile in a blue blur in Knuckles' direction. But it did no good. Sonic watched the grim echidna gracefully sidestep the threat. And that left it nowhere else to go but . . .

KRA-KOOOOOOM!

The missile exploded directly at the base of the owl statue. The whole room shook. For once, everything around Sonic was a blur in a bad way. The only thing he could clearly see was the statue as it collapsed and shattered into nothing but dust. A thousand years of history gone. And it was all his fault.

"Stuff it, Eggman!!" Sonic roared. As electric blue energy crackled about him, he spun into a furious ball and launched himself directly at Robotnik. Sonic ricocheted between the drones, unfurled his body, and grabbed a wide piece of drone shell, slicing it into the scientist's instruments. Then he blasted off the new egg-pod and toward a hole in the ceiling.

"Tails! Come on!" he called as he burst through a final sheet of thin ice and into the open air.

Tails soon zipped out overhead, flying down the mountain a heartbeat ahead of the villains. But Sonic had a better idea. Landing his red sneakers squarely in the center of his drone-shell weapon, he turned it into a makeshift snowboard. Sonic shredded his way down the mountain at top speed.

Sonic looked back to see a fleet of drones pouring out of the hole. Holding the compass, he knew they'd never let him go without a fight. Through the wind and snow, he could just make out the red form of Knuckles— cold and cruel as always. The echidna had crunched his own slice of shell into a board and was now cruising down the mountain in wordless fury.

"Has anyone ever told you you've got real anger issues?" the hedgehog called out.

"Surrender the compass! You stand no chance against me!" Knuckles was gaining on him now. "I've been training for this my entire life!"

"I have no training at all, and yet here I am ahead of you." Sonic waved the compass in a taunt. "That must be so embarrassing!"

The two began to sway back and forth

along the slope in a wicked cat-and-mouse chase. The echidna started digging his fists into the mountainside to push himself closer and closer. Trees and boulders alike fell as he dug his way right on top of Sonic.

"Up here!" Tails called from above Sonic's head.

The hedgehog tossed the compass up toward his partner, and it floated in his vision as if in slow motion . . . until Robotnik swiped it away! "Later, haters!" he cackled, and piloted his way into another deep crevasse. They followed as fast as they could.

In the cave they continued their ski-slope-style battle, accelerating the pace of the back and forth. Tails took off after Robotnik.

"Give up, fox, before I stuff your tails and hang them on my wall!" Robotnik jeered his way around columns of stone.

"Sorry, you're breaking up!" Tails mocked the villain, almost like Sonic would have. "I think your tech has a glitch!" With a few quick button mashes on one of his tool belt's endless gadget supply, the kid managed to remotely take control of the egg-pod!

"Welcome to Tails Mountain," the fox said, mimicking a theme park host as he guided Eggman around like a pinball. "For your safety, please keep your arms, legs, and creepy facial hair inside the ride at all times!" In a final move, Tails twisted the pod upside down and collected the compass as it fell from Robotnik's hands!

"What have you done to my baby?" the scientist screamed. "You think you can outsmart me? I'm the outsmarter! Nobody outsmarts the outsmarter!" And with the flick of a button, a volley of missiles erupted through the cave. One finally blew up next to Tails!

"Tails, no!" Sonic cried, still taking a pummeling from Knuckles' big fists.

An unconscious Tails crashed into the snow, compass sliding out of his hand. Both rolled down the slope of the mountain, getting closer and closer to a sharp drop off a cliff! Sonic couldn't lose his new friend *and* the only key to the Master Emerald! He had to get them back at all costs.

Sonic and Knuckles rode their boards inches from each other, their eyes locked on the compass. They both burst out of the mountain at top speed. But just before Sonic could break away, a stray boulder barreled out of the cave and struck his satchel. The bag flopped open, spilling his collection of rings across the snow and down into darkness!

Sonic regained his footing just in time to see Knuckles reaching out for the compass. They were all just at the cliff's edge, and the hedgehog had to make the most difficult decision of his life: save the compass or save Tails. It really wasn't a choice at all.

"Gah!" he cried, and swung one arm out for the fox and dug another into the snow for stability. Sonic had his friend. Tails wasn't moving, but he was breathing. He was okay— for now. The weight of two creatures slowed down the rapidly fraying snowboard to a stop, just inches from peril.

Sonic heard something coming down the mountain behind them.

Rrrrrrrrrrumble!

It was an avalanche!

"Enjoy the powder!" laughed Robotnik as the scientist grasped Knuckles *and* the compass in his egg-pod.

"Tails! Wake up! You gotta fly us outta here!" Sonic screamed into the fox's ear, but there was no response. Sonic reached into the satchel that flapped in the wind over his shoulder. No luck! In the fight, he'd dropped *all* his rings! Not a single warp portal was in his hands now. All he had left was a phone . . . the thing Robotnik had used to track them down.

What good could a phone do when they were about to be buried alive?

CHAPTER 11

Tom was feeling great. The sun glistened on the gorgeous Hawaiian beach. Maddie beamed as the maid of honor for her sister. And there were plenty of those great drinks in the coconut cups with the little umbrellas. The problems of Green Hills were hundreds of miles away.

Sure, there had been a few weird vibes over the weekend. Despite traveling by magic ring portal, Tom was feeling a little jet-lagged. Maddie's sister still hated him. And to top it off, there was something odd about the groomsmen. Four buff dudes in matching tuxedos and black wraparound shades kept staring him down like they shared one brain.

Whatever. Tom wasn't going to let it bother him. He'd done his one and only job for the wedding. He'd held the wedding rings for the morning and then tied them onto the little pillow Maddie's niece carried as she walked up the aisle. Easy peasy. Now all he had to do for the rest of the weekend was get another little coconut cup and watch the sun set into the ocean.

"And now, if we may have the rings?" asked the priest.

The ring bearer lifted the pillow up toward the bride and groom. The dearly beloved assembled in paradise held their breaths. It was perfect.

Twee-diddle-twee-diddle! Twee-diddle-twee-diddle!

Tom's phone rang, shattering the perfect moment. The bride shot him daggers.

"My bad!" Tom whispered at everyone. "I thought it was on silent!"

Hadn't it been? Tom suddenly realized that only the emergency calls he'd set up for Sonic would ring that loudly no matter what, and he dove behind a nearby bush to answer. Crouching low, Tom swiped the screen live to a video call.

"This better be an emergency, Sonic! I just . . . Are you skiing?!" Tom saw snow whip across Sonic's face as mountains flew by behind him. And was he holding an animal?

"Please, I need your help!" his hedgehog

ward shouted. "Life or death stuff right now, Tom!"

"What is going on?!"

"I need you to use that ring I gave you to save me—right now!"

"I don't even know where you are, Sonic!" Tom whisper-shouted, and prayed that the wedding party couldn't hear him through the foliage.

"You just gotta picture where you want the ring to go," Sonic said before waving his phone around, revealing a massive avalanche pouring toward them. "Picture this!!"

"Hold on!" Tom reached into his pocket and ran toward the beach. He tossed the single gold ring he had on his body into the air and thought of the horrifying scene on the phone . . .

And nothing happened.

"Did you throw it?" Sonic's voice yelled urgently from the phone.

Tom reached down and picked up the very ordinary wedding ring off the ground. "Oh man!" he said. "The warp ring must have gotten mixed up with the wedding rings while I was holding them!"

"Then where is it now, Tom?!"

Tom realized the ring was in the worst possible place ever. It was about to be put onto Rachel's finger.

"Hold tight! I got this!" he yelled to Sonic, and then slowly reentered the wedding, walking up the aisle.

"Excuse me! I need to see that ring," Tom yelled out.

The entire wedding turned their heads toward him.

"Tom, I'm going to kill you," Rachel said

with a scary look in her eyes.

"Tom, what are you doing?!" Maddie said.

Undeterred, Tom walked up to the altar.

"I need that ring."

"Tom, please sit down," said Randall, the groom.

"I'm sorry," Tom said, and he punched Randall in the face, the ring flying from his hand.

Tom snatched the ring out of the air and in an instant tossed it.

Zam!

A portal opened in the middle of the aisle, and it immediately spewed out a metric ton of snow right into the faces of the four men. They collapsed under its icy weight as the crowd screamed.

When the portal's light faded away, Tom saw that Sonic had landed on top of the snow mound that now occupied half the wedding stage.

In the madness, Tom and Maddie both rushed to Sonic's side.

"Sonic! Are you okay?!" he said.

"What's happening? Are you hurt?" Maddie asked.

"I'm—I'm fine," Sonic said, totally not fine.

"Okay, good," Tom exhaled, and then sucked in a breath to scream out, "because you are SO GROUNDED! No screen time for a year! For TEN YEARS!"

"Tom, listen to me," Sonic said with a more earnest look than any the kid had ever given him. "Robotnik is back on Earth, and he's after a magic Emerald! The only way to find it is with a special compass that Robotnik has *right now*! So Tails and I need to get it back or the world is doomed!"

"All of this happened since yesterday?" Maddie asked.

Sonic reached into the pile of snow and pulled out the still-breathing body of what looked like a fox, but a humanoid, like Sonic. The kid groaned as Sonic turned him over, and Tom noticed two wet tails hanging off Sonic's arm.

"Tails? Can you hear me?" Sonic said, and shook the fox gently.

Tom kneeled down and put his arm around the pair. "Don't worry, Sonic. We'll get him help. We'll solve this."

"How about *we* take it from here?" came a voice from behind them. Tom turned and saw a figure coming down the aisle toward him. He wore a Hawaiian shirt but walked like a soldier. This guy definitely wasn't on the wedding's guest list.

"Wait, I know you!" Tom realized. "You're that Department of Defense spook who showed up last year after the battle in Green Hills. The one who left us that high-tech walkie-talkie."

"Correct!" the man said. "Though I may have misled you on my credentials. My name is Commander Walters, and I represent the Guardian Units of Nations—a global task force created after the incident in San Francisco and dedicated to protecting Earth from alien threats." He flashed a badge with a spiked G at its center.

"Wait a minute . . . your organization is an acronym . . . for G.U.N.?!" Maddie said. "Who would call a spy organization G.U.N.? That doesn't even sound real!"

"It's totally real!" Walters snapped. "And as a federal agent, I'm calling jurisdiction on this site. We knew you were harboring this hedgehog creature, Wachowski, but we never thought you'd hand him over. So we had to set up this sting operation to draw him out of hiding."

"Sting operation?" Tom said, and then he realized . . . the groomsmen with the mystery blasters who were currently buried under a pile of snow. They were G.U.N. agents. That meant that the groom . . .

"You're a secret agent and you didn't tell me?!" the bride screamed, and began to beat her partner mercilessly.

"That's correct," Walters said. "The priest, the wedding band . . . even the groom! Every aspect of Operation Catfish was a complete fabrication. We had to ensure these alien threats were contained."

Slowly, arms began to move from within

the snow mound. The "groomsmen" had come to and were rising to circle around Sonic and Tails, blasters ready.

"Tom?" Sonic called, clutching the fox tighter.

"You're making a mistake!" Tom called, and began to slug every agent in sight. A slippery wrestling match ensued, but before Tom could fight them all off, one leveled a blaster at Sonic, and *WHOOOM!* A laser net shot out, capturing the two aliens in its webbing. Tom screamed before two agents collapsed on him, wrestling him into a pair of handcuffs.

"Sonic isn't a threat! He's on our side!" Maddie pleaded with the commander. "You should be protecting the planet from Doctor Robotnik!"

"Robotnik is dead," Walters sneered.

"You're wrong. He's back. And you've just captured the only ones who can stop him!"

Commander Walters paused and then slowly spoke into a wrist communicator. "Sounds like Doctor Robotnik might be back in play. If he is, I want him found immediately!" he said. "And get me a helicopter evac for Wachowski and these aliens—immediately!"

The G.U.N. agents dragged Tom to his feet and pulled along Sonic and Tails like they were common animals and not the world's only hope. Tom looked into Maddie's eyes, powerless.

CHAPTER 12

Robotnik's brain was on fire with the possibilities before him. Below, the roaring waves of the avalanche were burying his hated enemy. In his grasp was the key to lead him to the Master Emerald and ultimate power. He was so close to achieving his dream of a world destroyed by chaos and then perfectly reorganized by his intelligent design.

"He chose saving the fox over his

compass," said Knuckles as he hung off the side of Robotnik's egg-pod.

"Of course he did." Robotnik brushed off his passenger's awe. "New friend, same pathetic weakness." Knuckles glared at him. "Which is completely unlike our friendship . . . one built on power and respect!" the doctor recovered quickly.

Knuckles turned the compass over in his hands. After pressing its center, a glowing globe spun to life in the air. It was a perfect jewel ready for the snatching—both the Emerald and this world.

"Tell me, my crimson companion . . . what's your endgame? What will you do with the power of the ultimate Chaos Emerald once it's in your swollen clutches, huh?" Robotnik fished for any additional info that could come in handy.

"I will return with the Emerald to my ancestral home, using its power to lift the capital temple of echidna society from the sinking ruin it's become and restore it to glory." The creature's eyes were fierce. "I warn you, I'm the last of my kind. The Master Emerald is my destiny. The only way to bring back my people."

"If that glowing orb of a compass is correct, this ring is our quickest path to the other side of the globe . . . where *your* Emerald awaits. Shall we?"

Knuckles reluctantly lifted a ring in the air and opened a portal to the South Pacific.

Zam!

They dropped from the portal and onto the peak of a tiny rock-covered island that jutted out of the Pacific Ocean. There was nothing else as far as the eye could see.

"This cannot be right," said Knuckles. "Have we misread the compass?"

"I don't misread. *Ever.* Look down."

Knuckles held out the compass, and its laser lights focused themselves on a point going straight down. Beneath their feet, a stone marker protruded out amid the craggy natural landscape. Robotnik hated nature and all it stood for, but at least this spot held the potential for the sweet, sterile power of alien tech.

The echidna dropped from the egg-pod and landed atop the marker. "The carvings here match the key system used by my ancestors," Knuckles said, fitting the compass into a wide divot in the stone.

Cha-Klang! Shoooooooooom!

With a turn of the compass key, the entire island began to rumble. A whirlpool began swirling around the tiny island, and the ocean seemed to drain away around them. It revealed a massive structure of stone extending far beneath them. And then . . . *Foom!* A ray of bright green light shot from Knuckles' marker and straight into the sky above.

"Holy Moses!" Robotnik cheered. "I've found it! Archimedes would be floating in his grave right now!" Knuckles' eyes were steely, and he only scanned the depths of the churning water. Seriously, what was the fun in upsetting the balance of all life on planet Earth if you couldn't gloat about it a little?

The pair grasped tightly to the peak of what was revealing itself to be a massive hidden structure. If the compass's resting place was an Owl Tribe temple, this location was practically the lost city of Atlantis.

"Not much impresses you, does it?" Robotnik called to his emotionless echidna.

"We should retrieve the Emerald now!" Without another thought, Knuckles jumped down into a crevasse on the still-rising island's rock face. Deep below, Robotnik could see the water draining from inside, and as he maneuvered his pod after the echidna, the details of an elaborate labyrinth came into focus.

His last remaining drones scanned the walls and fed him data on the underground maze. It was disgusting. Mossy living things. Carving after carving of majestic owls . . . those grotesque, pellet-pooping monstrosities. The walls of the labyrinth were a monument to wild, living things—the kinds of things his bots would someday replace with cold, metallic perfection.

The pathways in the labyrinth narrowed. Stinking, static water still pooled around Knuckles' feet, but the creature dug forward with purpose. At this point, even Robotnik was beginning to lose his place.

"Hey, Knucklehead!" he called. "I know you're dying to get your Emerald on, but could we be a little more mindful? A crumbling animal cage like this usually contains booby traps, and I've only got three drones left!"

K-tang! Crshhhhhhh!

A spear flew out of a side wall and cleaved a drone in half. Its finely tuned circuits spat hot sparks as its oil-hemorrhaging body crashed into the water below.

"Make that *two* drones!"

"Fear not, friend," Knuckles said without looking back. "In a moment, I'll have my

Emerald, and balance will be restored to the Echidna Tribe *and* the universe."

Click!

At that moment, he stepped on a pressure plate in the floor, setting off a series of booby-trap blades that sliced, diced, and dissected everything in the tunnel they could reach. Robotnik pushed his egg-pod ahead, tossing Knuckles into an open chamber just as the last of the blades chopped another of his drones in half.

"You see what I mean?!" the scientist cried before briefly regaining his composure. "Allow me to show you how you can work smarter, not harder."

With a tap on his control pad, Robotnik commanded his last remaining drone to scan deeper into the rock of the labyrinth. In minutes, the computer had calculated every turn, tunnel, and trap in the place. It would be slow going, and Robotnik would have to stoop to traveling on foot. But they'd get there alive if his companion could hold his dang horses for once.

It took hours. They pressed deeper and deeper into the muck and mold of the hot and humid labyrinth until, with a glowing super punch, Knuckles broke through a stone wall and into the structure's main chamber. And as the dust settled, there it was amid the gloom. Floating in the middle of the grand cavern . . . the green Master Emerald!

"At last!" Knuckles called.

"Ultimate power . . . ," Robotnik said, grinning.

"Soon, order will be restored. Peace will be everlasting . . . all because of what we've done together."

"Aww, such a lovely sentiment, Knuckles. I believe I feel a single tear forming," Robotnik said as he snuck up behind the creature. Now was the moment to strike. The echidna was no longer of any use. In fact, he was the only thing standing between Robotnik and total domination.

CHAPTER 13

In intergalactic animal society, there was no crime greater than keeping a creature bound in a cage. And despite years as an outsider to his own kind, Tails had never known this unique pain until he faded into consciousness somewhere warm—far and away from the wind and snow in Siberia.

As soon as Tails understood what he was being carried in, he faded back into a painful slumber. Was this all a dream? Had he even met his hero? Or maybe he was just the crazy freak everyone back home said he was.

"Come on! You can't just leave us here! My friend is hurt. He needs a doctor . . . a vet . . . anyone!" a voice called out like a dream. In a nearby cage of his own, Sonic the Hedgehog called out to the wounded fox to no avail. "Tails, come on. You gotta wake up!"

"Poor little guy," came the gentle voice of a man that must have been Sonic's ally. "Who is he?"

"His name is Tails, Tom. He's a genius. Brave. He came all the way to this world to find me . . . Tails is a lot like I was when I first came to Earth. All alone on a strange planet. Needing to find someone to believe in. A hero. Only I got lucky. I found Donut Lord. All Tails found was . . . me. Only Sonic the Hedgehog could have let him down this much." Tails could hear the pain and tears in Sonic's voice. Maybe this *wasn't* just a bad dream?

"Listen, Sonic. You didn't just find Donut Lord," Tom said. "Donut Lord didn't even exist until I found *you*. Until I finally found out how it felt to be responsible for someone other than myself. That's what growing up is all about, pal."

The room that the three of them sat in came into focus: a small holding cell full of baggage. Tails weakly whispered the first thought on his mind. "The Emerald . . ." barely passed his lips when his world was rocked again.

BOOM!

The doors blew off the holding room as Sonic and Tom both shouted, "Maddie!"

In the smoldering hole, a human woman stood. Around her waist was Tails' tool belt. It was a good fit. "Come on," Maddie said. "We're busting out of here!"

"You're amazing, you know that?" Tom kissed her after she removed his handcuffs. "How did you pull this off?"

"It wasn't too tough. Been working my way with a little alien tech," she said, showing off a few of Tails' miniature explosives. "Whoever's responsible for these things really saved the day."

"That's this guy here. We call him Tails."

Maddie knelt down by Tails' cage and reached gently. "He's got a pulse, but it's weak," she said. "We need to move. Follow me, but this whole hotel is crawling with G.U.N. agents. I can target them with Tails' devices. That seems to be working so far."

Maddie sprinted into the hallway like a righteous warrior. She activated a pulse ray to lift furniture up off the ground and bowl over agents! In a flash, another gizmo magnetized their weapons, pulling the blasters out of G.U.N. hands and away from danger. She even snapped out bolo whips that tangled and tripped new waves of attackers.

Free of his cage, Sonic bounced from agent to agent as Tom sprinted along in their wake, cradling Tails' carrier. The group made their way to the exit, cut off by a final pair of burly G.U.N. agents. Maddie whipped out her last defensive device: a gumball-size black ball with only the barest hint of a switch on the outside. She pressed it but then held on . . . her first wrong choice!

"Get . . . rid of it . . . ," Tails called, but his voice was unheard in the chaos.

Beep-beep-beeeeeeeeeeeep!

"What's that supposed to mean? Beeping is bad!" Maddie said as the final wave of agents ran at them. "Sorry for whatever's about to happen to you!" she said, and threw it right at them.

Fwump!

Suddenly, the ball burst into a massive wave of goo that quickly hardened around the agents, holding them fast against the wall. "This is gross." Maddie shrugged. "More for you guys than me, but still."

They ran outside toward the beach— anywhere that was away from their pursuers. Sonic picked up speed as they got back to the now deserted site of the wedding reception.

"Not so fast!" came a harsh military voice.

"This guy again?" Sonic groaned.

"Don't roll your eyes at G.U.N.

Commander Walters," the man said in a pompous tone. "As soon as my men recover from your shenanigans and get these aliens into the hands of our scientists, I'll be up for a promotion. Maybe even the presidency. Why not? I worked for it."

"How about you work your way through this?!" Maddie shouted, and tossed the final goo bomb in her arsenal at him.

Walters dodged it. "Well, you forgot the first rule of warfare: Never bring a ball of exploding alien goo to a G.U.N. fight!"

"Oh, this little lady brought a gun," Maddie said, and through the haze, Tails knew what she meant and felt afraid. It was the piece of his tool belt even he wasn't sure should be used. "It's just a very little gun. Sonic . . . think fast!"

Maddie flipped something off the end of

the belt, and it flew into the air. Bouncing off a table, Sonic tipped the gizmo midair until it fell squarely into Tom's hands. It was a gun . . . sort of? Probably only big enough to really fit in Tails' hand. But Tom aimed it with every ounce of focus his small-town sheriff training provided him.

"Hands up, Walters!" Tom shouted.

"As if that squirt gun is anything compared to the authority my badge empowers me with!"

Zyark!!! The blaster shot went wide and completely atomized the wedding cake.

"Okay, so maybe it's something compared to my badge." Walters cowered, hands up.

"Hey, Tom?" Sonic whispered. "Do us all a favor and be careful with that."

The team tied up Walters, but they were running out of time.

"How can we find where the compass was leading them without Tails?" Sonic asked his family.

FOOOOOOOM! Far out on the ocean, a bright beacon of green light split the sky in two.

"Well, that works, I guess," Sonic said before shaking his head in dismay. "The compass has led them to the Emerald already."

"As bright as that light is, it's still got to be miles away on the open ocean. We'll never get there in time," Maddie said.

"*We* won't," Tom added. "But *you* can, Sonic."

"Me? No way. You don't know this Knuckles guy. He's stronger than me, tougher than me—not as handsome, sure, but no one is the total package." Sonic sighed. "I can't do this, Tom. I'm just a kid!"

"No, you're not 'just a kid,' Sonic," Tom said, kneeling down. "Remember the last time you fought Robotnik? What did you say?"

"That his facial hair looked super creepy?"

"Not that. The other thing."

"I said that this is my power, and I'm going to use it to protect my friends."

"That's right . . . because that's what a hero does," Tom said finally. "And if you keep ahold of that in your heart, there's nothing you can't do."

Donut Lord was right! As Sonic hugged them goodbye and dug in for a run across the ocean, Tails realized he had to be a hero, too. He had to shake off his wounds. If he couldn't help Sonic now, no one could. Clearing his mind of the haze, the fox started kicking at the door of his carrying cage just as Sonic zoomed into the distance.

"No, wait!" Tails finally called, though his voice was hoarse. "Don't go, Sonic! I'm coming with you! You need . . ." But he was already gone—just the trail of a blue electric blur on the horizon.

"Hey, hey, little guy. Calm down," Tom said, wrapping an arm around Tails' shoulder. "You can't go after Sonic. You're hurt."

"But we have to help him," Tails said firmly, his strength seeming to grow back inside of him. "You don't know what he's up against. He can't do this alone."

CHAPTER 14

The water skittered underneath his sneakers, spewing out a massive spray in his wake. Steam mixed in as the friction of his feet boiled the ocean's surface like a pot on a stove. He always wondered if he could go fast enough to run on water. Now he knew. But he knew as well that one fall would see him crash beneath the waves . . . and he still couldn't swim.

But he had to push forward now on his

own. He'd make it up to Tails for leaving the fox behind. He wasn't trying to do it all alone anymore, but he just didn't have a choice.

"Gotta go fast!" Sonic said as he pushed himself harder, covering the miles to that distant light in a matter of moments.

The wine-dark sea swelled angrily as he came closer and closer to the beacon. The green light poured out of the peak of a tiny rocky island. With the waves swirling around it, Sonic's tenuous balancing act was thrown for a loop. With each new step, his feet sunk just below the surface of the water before he launched off again. His balance became unsteady. The waters rose in violent waves.

And just as he reached the edge of the island's whirlpool, he finally made a fatal slip. For the first time in his life, Sonic lost his footing underneath him. He hit the water at over three hundred miles an hour, face-first! Like a skipping stone, Sonic skidded off the surface and into the air. His head took the brunt of the blow . . . until finally everything went black.

When he came to, Sonic was sure that he was at the bottom of a watery grave. But then he heard the gentle sound of water lapping at the shore. He opened his eyes, and despite a pretty major pain in his neck, he seemed okay. Sonic struggled to his feet only to realize that hard rock stood beneath him. He was on the island. He'd made it!

From this vantage point, he saw how the ocean created a massive bowl of space, and in the midst of it all was not just an island but a temple city! With the green light of the beacon bursting forth from its summit just behind Sonic's head, the temple seemed to go on forever deep into the earth below.

And if that's where Robotnik and Knuckles had gone, it's where he would go, too.

Sonic jumped down the closest hole he could and plummeted into darkness. His feet hit a slick patch of stone, and suddenly Sonic was riding down a chute of pouring water. He set out his hands and surfed his way down and out over the edge of a waterfall, launching off the lip of the spout just in time to avoid another swim trap.

He landed in a gigantic room—clearly the entry to the labyrinth. A giant owl statue loomed above his head. Longclaw's tribe hid the Emerald here who knows how many years ago, but the real question was "Which way?" From the opening, Sonic could tell there were many paths. But he couldn't assume that all of them would take him to the Master Emerald.

"Okay, trial and error . . . ," Sonic said, and sprinted down a first path. It immediately collapsed beneath him, and Sonic hopped back just in time to avoid a pit of spikes! "That was an error."

He'd be more cautious on take two, feeling his way down another path. That is, he thought he could go easy, until his foot set off a pressure plate that launched a volley of arrows right at his head!

"Zero for two. Rough start," Sonic said after ducking out of danger. "I don't have time for this!"

If caution wouldn't yield results, Sonic had to do what he did best: rush in as fast as possible and try not to get killed. He was the fastest thing alive, after all. Why should some labyrinth of booby traps trip him up?

What followed was a flurry of action

as Sonic made a speed run at every tunnel available. Some ramps collapsed halfway through his run, and Sonic had to spin jump to safety. Deep in the bowels of one path, he narrowly avoided a spiked wrecking ball. Down at the lowest levels, the stonework of the labyrinth fell sharply into rivers of flowing lava. Sonic could ride them for a while until the blocks were eaten up by the hot magma. But even after all that, he still hadn't found the Emerald.

Then, at last, he broke through. Swinging on a tangled seaweed vine over the worst of the booby traps, Sonic kicked his way through a crumbling wall and into a central chamber. The green glow of the Emerald and its beacon radiated in the room's center.

"Nailed it." Sonic laughed to himself, but he soon realized he was not alone. Across the chamber, Knuckles and Robotnik stood side by side. Apparently, they'd just made it through themselves.

"Isn't there always someone trying to ruin a bad thing?" Robotnik cried out.

"Oh, you guys are here, too?" Sonic said, squaring off against Knuckles as the Master Emerald shimmered just beyond the reach of them all. "You must've taken the long way, huh?"

"Enough!" Knuckles hollered in rage. "How many times must I destroy you in one day?"

"I don't die so easily, Knucklehead!" Sonic laughed, but behind him, he felt a familiar rumble from his speed run through the labyrinth's many zones.

Sha-Booooom!

A giant spiked wrecking ball burst

through the wall behind them, demolishing the support pillars of the room. "Oh, I was wondering where that went," Sonic said with a smile before leaping out of its path.

"Is everything a big joke to you?" Knuckles growled. "Why do you constantly insist on interfering with my destiny?"

"I don't believe in destiny. But I do believe in my friends. And my family. And more importantly . . . they believe in me," said Sonic.

Robotnik blanched. "I think I just threw up in my mouth."

The wrecking ball ricocheted off the columns of the chamber, breaking stone to rubble as it went. The room shook violently, and Sonic made a dash toward the Emerald, leaping from fallen stone to fallen stone. But just as he was within reaching distance of the prize, *Wham*! Knuckles charged into him with full force and launched Sonic across the room.

"Boy, you two really want to hurt each other," Robotnik called. "Are you sure you're not related?"

Now it was Knuckles' turn to go for the Master Emerald. He rushed forward fists-first like an ape charging through the jungle. Sonic whipped himself into a spin attack and cut the echidna off midway, blasting both combatants back to opposite sides of the chamber.

The hedgehog steadied himself, while across the cavern, Knuckles dug his fists into the ground, equally ready for a bull rush. The Emerald would have to wait until these two settled the score.

"You've interfered with my destiny for the last time, hedgehog!" Knuckles yelled.

"Aw, really?" Sonic said cheerfully. "That's too bad. I was enjoying kicking your butt."

Sonic dove into the space above, his chaotic speed energy rippling off him in electric blue waves. When Knuckles leaped up to meet him, an angry wave of red energy followed in his wake. The two met in a colorful clash of muscle and magic. The temple began to collapse around them from their battle, but they were too focused—and too evenly matched—to notice or care.

"Why don't you stand still and die with honor?" Knuckles howled.

"Another idea: How about I run around a lot, and you don't kill me?"

Amid the madness, a sneaking presence crept ever closer to the Emerald. Robotnik didn't have his army of drones on him now, but that didn't make him any less dangerous.

"Hey there, beautiful," he said, approaching the gem. "You're the real deal, aren't you?"

"Knuckles, stop!" cried Sonic, seeing the danger too late. "Robotnik is stealing the Emerald!"

"What kind of fool do you take me for?"

"JUST LOOK!!!"

The echidna turned just in time to see his worst fears realized. An unworthy villain had latched onto the Master Emerald, screaming "Mine!" And with that single touch, the powers of all the seven legendary Chaos Emeralds of old were reborn in him. The Master Emerald embedded itself in Robotnik's chest, merging with the madman.

"Wait!" called Knuckles. "That wasn't the deal. I trusted you. You were my friend!"

"Oh, you poor naive creature." Robotnik laughed as green energy pulsated all over his body. "A more advanced intellect would have seen this move coming. And anyway, I told you no matter who you think your new friend is . . . friendship as a construct is still pathetic!"

"Dishonor!" Knuckles screamed in rage.

Now fully transforming into a glowing, giddy being of pure chaos, Robotnik lifted an arm and shot a force blast high through the ceiling. He flew skyward—no drones needed—and rippled with green energy that could remake the world. As his creepy laughter rang through the chamber, the columns began to collapse around Sonic and Knuckles.

CHAPTER 15

Sonic had no other choice. The stonework of the chamber was falling like rain now, and if he didn't want his face to be smashed to pieces, he'd have to go down. All the way into the water below. Sonic splashed hard at the edge of the black waves, looking for a way out.

Amid the falling debris, Sonic noticed the echidna had been pinned down by a massive stone column. He struggled to pull his leg free but couldn't make the column budge.

"He betrayed me," Knuckles grunted as Sonic ran up.

"Of course. He's Ro-Butt-Nik. That's what he does!" Sonic threw his arms up in the air. "And now he has the Emerald. I hope you're happy."

"Why would I be happy? This is a horrible outcome!"

The falling stones settled, but it was far from the end of their troubles. Without the Master Emerald in place, the labyrinth had no other option but to sink back into the ocean. As it sank, the chamber began to flood—bubbling water rising in every nook and cranny. Sonic started to speed around the perimeter, looking for a way out. Across the chamber, one hole opened up to the sky and safety. He could run out now, but even after all that had happened, he couldn't just leave Knuckles behind. "Let's get out of here!" he called.

Knuckles tried in vain to bench-press the column, but he finally dropped his arms, out of breath.

"What are you doing?!" Sonic said, kicking at the column in panic.

"I spent my whole life training for this. And I failed."

CRUSH! Another stone block fell on top of the column, double pinning the echidna down. Knuckles smiled weakly. "A fitting end for a failure."

"You're not a failure," Sonic said. "You're a fighter. So fight!"

"Let me die in peace, pest."

The murky liquid rose over the echidna's head. A few last bubbles floated to its surface as Sonic screamed, "Knuckles!!!" Sonic sucked in the biggest breath he could possibly hold and dove deep into the black water.

Sonic tried to push the stone—too heavy! About to lose his breath, he noticed a series of large bubbles pushing up through the cracks in the chamber floor. Sonic took a drastic move and pushed his face into a bubble—and it worked!

He went back to his adversary a second time, pleading with Knuckles, who finally relented. The echidna put his hands on the column, and they pushed together.

The force of both warriors together was enough to give an inch of room, and Knuckles wriggled free. He immediately pulled his arms up in a forceful paddling motion and began to rise to the surface. But Sonic still didn't know how to swim. Faltering in the water, he sank and saw the red warrior floating farther and farther away from him. In the end, Sonic felt that he was all alone . . . sinking to the bottom of the sea.

But before the darkness settled in, a massive, knuckled white glove reached down and grabbed Sonic by the arm. It pulled him up, out, and to the water's surface.

The sky was dark, and a sliver of moon lit the night. Around them, the space that had once been a massive whirlpool was now just dark, choppy water, and the craggy island temple that housed the labyrinth was once again fully submerged except for the simple stone peak that barely stood above the water's surface. A piece of rotted driftwood rose up from the depths, and they grabbed on for dear life.

"Why did you save me?" Knuckles asked

as he continued to swim toward the island's tip. "I've been trying to destroy you since the moment I laid eyes on you."

"Because . . . I don't know. I couldn't just let you die."

"Why? You wish to destroy me, too."

"Uh . . . what are you talking about?"

"You were raised by the murderous owls. From the day I was born, I was told they were savages—Barbarians!—and that the fate of the world depended on stopping them and protecting the Emerald. Then the day came to fight them, but my father stopped me from joining the battle. He said my time to honor our tribe would come . . . but I was only a child."

"You were trying to grow up too fast . . ." Sonic shook his head.

"Those were the last words he said to me. I

never saw him again because your people are killers!"

"Ahhh!" Sonic found himself slipping off the wood.

"But you're not . . . are you?" Knuckles slowly realized how wrong he'd had it. It took him long enough!

"The only place I kill it is on the dance floor." Sonic laughed.

But Knuckles was in no laughing mood. "My whole life has been a lie."

"I don't think so. Your whole life, you've been training to do the right thing . . . you just didn't know exactly what that was. You thought we were enemies, but we're in the same boat."

"My punches must have damaged your brain." Knuckles chuckled at last. "We are not in a boat."

"I'm saying we both want to protect the Emerald," Sonic explained. "And I think, if we work together, we can do it."

"Stop talking." The echidna shook him off.

"I'm serious. A wise old man with a breakfast-pastry obsession once told me that everyone needs help—that the way to be a hero is to find your team of people like you who can—"

"Hedgehog, be silent for once in your life! I hear something . . ."

Sonic stopped and heard it, too. It was an engine—an old-timey biplane buzzing along in the distance. And it was headed right for them.

"That sly little fox," Sonic said to himself.

Tails, decked out in aviator goggles and a flowing scarf, waved a hand as he circled close to where they were. Off the back of the plane, a banner from the ruined wedding reception dropped and allowed them to climb aboard. Now all they had to do was chase down the most dangerous man in the universe.

CHAPTER 16

"Chaos IS POWER!!!!"

Robotnik's words echoed off the clouds in the sky like a prophecy coming true. He could see it all so clearly now. With the power of the Master Emerald absorbed into his body, he no longer needed satellites or drones or bootlickers to control the world around him. He could reach out and touch the world in a way no living being ever had.

The universe itself was a brain. His brain. His big, giant, pulsating brain.

Coasting over the Pacific Ocean, Robotnik hit the western United States with a vengeance. As he pushed his energized form past the dopey little mud huts mankind called civilization, the doctor called every bit of tech to him. Even the smallest circuits and spark plugs were his to command now.

And he knew just where to start.

>>>>>>>>

Crouching low in the bushes near the café was the chief mouth breather of all creation, Deputy Sheriff Wade. The moron stammered as he called his big boss man hero for help.

"Tom! It's Robotnik! He's back!"

"Yeah, I know that already," Tom said from a plane still miles away.

"Oh. I wish you'd told me," said Wade with a shrug. "I guess you know he's got a secret lair inside the Mean Bean, too."

"He what?!?!" Tom shouted. "Wade, don't move, okay? I'll be there as soon as I can. Do NOT go in there!"

"What? You want me to go in there!" Wade misheard not because of high dropped call rates in Montana but because Robotnik created interference. Like a darling DJ, he skipped and scratched the audio track of Wachowski's call to dupe the dunderhead into danger.

"Wade, d . . . go in there! Do you hear me? Do *kshhh!* go in there!" Tom's voice garbled its way into the deputy's ear.

"All right . . . Sheriff for the weekend, going in!" Wade responded, and ran into the Mean Bean, weapon drawn. If Robotnik was lucky, either he or Stone would dispatch the other. A terrific cosmic joke on the pair of them.

But swatting at flies brought him no great pleasure. If Robotnik were to claim ultimate triumph, he'd need to smash the lawman even worse than he'd done to that drowning blue hedgehog miles behind him. And so Robotnik zeroed his chaotic master mind on Tom's whereabouts, keeping one step ahead of the do-gooders.

"Do you believe me now?" Tom asked the commander of the high-speed plane they currently occupied.

"This is Commander Walters . . . Scramble every available piece of hardware to Green

Hills, Montana, immediately!" the G.U.N. overlord ordered. "We've got a Code Mustache. I repeat: CODE MUSTACHE!"

Let them try and come for him. Robotnik was not simply a man anymore. He was all men just as he was no men, and therefore he was . . . a god. It felt like a chorus of dancing girls were continually backing him up as he kicked off the shackles of mortality. It was funky.

In the mostly insignificant instants between when Robotnik spied on his enemies and when he arrived in Green Hills, the sheriff's idiot partner had managed to hog-tie Agent Stone to a chair. But as Robotnik touched down in the parking lot of the secret base, he knew they'd soon be feeding his massive ego or be crushed by it . . . as was intended.

"Doctor!" cried Stone like an infant as Robotnik glided to the ground, still surging with power. "Sir, are . . . are you feeling okay?"

"OKAY??" Robotnik swiveled his head unit to the right exactly forty-five degrees and beheld his inferior. "I am more than okay," he declared in glee. "I have upgraded. I've taken my game to the next level. It's a hybrid of chess and quantum leapfrog. Wanna play?"

In a flash, Robotnik converted his body into energy and then reconstituted himself behind Stone like a bit of binary code flickering one to zero and back again. Teleportation was just a parlor trick to him now.

"Check!" he called out as he undid Stone's handcuffs without touching them.

"I can smell the electricity in your brain . . . a fine, robust meal for my new form," he said to his underling before turning to his idiot adversary. "You smell like a snack plate."

"Kinda my mom's specialty," Wade stammered.

"Sir," Stone called from the view screen. "We've got a problem."

"Incorrect, my trusty sycophant," Robotnik droned. "After all these years, what I've finally got is a solution."

The mad genius raised the shutters of the café's windows and revealed a sight Stone cowered from: an assembled battalion of commandos from G.U.N.

They were head to toe in bulletproof armor, packing the most technologically advanced blasters this side of a sci-fi movie. And they were backed by a fleet of tanks, choppers, and cannons. In other words, they were easy pickings for the power of the Master Emerald.

Robotnik blew through the window and into the street. The soldiers were shaking in their boots, he could tell. But they weren't the ones he wanted to dismantle first. And if calculations were correct (as they of course were), then the object of his ire would just be arriving at the back of the battlements— flown direct from Hawaii in an out-of-date stealth jet.

"Wade?!" called Tom, arriving on the scene.

"Well, well, well . . . if it isn't the Pastry King," the doctor taunted.

"It's Donut Lord," Tom snapped back. "A real genius would remember the name of the guy who helped kick your scrawny butt off this planet. And I'll do it again if you mess with Green Hills." His tender-hearted paramour stepped out from behind him and with . . . a face from the doctor's past.

"You're finished, Robotnik," barked G.U.N. Commander Walter. "We've taken everything. Your lab. Your drones. Your funding. Let's see how big of a man you are without your silly little robots."

"You want to see how *big* of a man I can be?" Robotnik laughed. He had them exactly where he wanted them.

Reaching out his fingertips and shooting energy into the air, Robotnik handily dismantled a G.U.N. tank. The soldiers inside fell through the air as its pieces swirled around Robotnik like perfectly balanced electrons orbiting an atom's nucleus.

"My god . . ." Walters gawked from below.

"Correct!" Robotnik cheered. "I AM your god!"

"Open fire! Light him up!" the commander called.

But it was too late. The soldiers' guns came apart in their hands, their metal components floating into the sphere around Robotnik.

The sphere grew larger and more impressive. The little people below were horrified to see what he was becoming. An egg-like cranium. Arms of steel. Bone-crunching boots. And a body of pure robotic might. The Master Emerald let Robotnik be anything and everything, and what he wanted to be most in the world was an all-domineering Giant Eggman Robot.

"Stone!" the doctor called to his henchman through the electronic ether. "If you want a chance of living through my impending re-creation of all existence, I demand you load up my World Domination playlist into my mech's earpiece this instant! I'm vibing!"

CHAPTER 17

Over the ocean, the horizon seemed
to go on forever with no land in sight, but
Tails had faith they'd make it back in time to
stop Robotnik. Normally, their flight would
have taken eight hours in an average human
transport. But it was cut to barely under
two, thanks to Tails' latest innovation. He'd
combined his magnetic thruster technology
with the light body of an old Earth biplane
and come up with . . . the Tornado.

Now the red plane crested over the continental United States with Sonic and Knuckles riding along. They were perhaps the only passengers who could withstand the gale-force winds that whipped across the low-flying aircraft as it shot toward Green Hills.

They were in the final leg now as Tails' guidance system pointed them toward Montana and into the shadow of an ominous storm cloud crackling with green lightning.

"The fearsome power of the Emerald," Knuckles said.

Tails whispered as best he could in his hero's direction. "Are you sure it was a bright idea bringing . . ." He jerked his head slightly in Knuckles' direction. "You-Know-Who aboard for this?"

"Knuckles isn't really a bad guy . . . He's just a little confused," Sonic reassured him.

"I am *not* confused!" Knuckles shouted over the sound of the wind. "I have steely focus."

Still cutting through the atmosphere at maximum velocity, Tails pulled up over the rolling country and into the heart of the town of Green Hills. None of them were prepared for what they saw.

Towering high above the buildings was a massive Robotnik. This mustache-twirling Giant Eggman Robot stomped through downtown, bursting buildings into flames as it went.

It was a revolting sight to see its steel skin shiver and morph into a stronger exterior with each new bit of technology that Robotnik pulled into his form.

Tails jerked the stick of the Tornado off to the side so he could make a wide sweep around the Giant Eggman Robot, looking for any weak spots. It seemed impossible.

Sonic took charge. "We need a plan. Knuckles, why don't you . . ."

"Yaaaaaaaaaaaaaaaaa!" The echidna jumped from his seat and flew through the air at their gigantic foe.

"Ugh. This guy is killing me!" Sonic climbed out onto the double wing of the plane and steadied himself for a different kind of assault. "Looks like it's gonna be just you and me, buddy. You up for it?"

"If I'm going to go out, Sonic . . . I'd want to do it alongside you."

"Don't get ahead of yourself." The hedgehog laughed. "Get us as close as you can. I'm going to try to—Tails, LOOK OUT!"

They'd been spotted, and a barrage of makeshift missiles flew out of the Giant Eggman Robot's body. With stolen gas tanks fueling them and makeshift metal warheads, these weren't as destructive as the average Robotnik missile. But Tails still needed to take evasive maneuvers and do barrel rolls to get them through without a scratch.

"That was close!" Sonic called when they were in the clear. But he was laughing. It was a mad, heroic laugh.

"I know, right?" Tails called back, laughing along. He found it infectious. For the first time in his life, he felt like he belonged . . . even if the place he belonged was on the verge of a crazy death.

WHOMP!

One last bit of jet-propelled shrapnel

shot out from the Giant Eggman Robot and knocked Sonic clear off the wing! Tails turned the plane toward the villain and busted out his ace in the hole: laser cannons powered by the same tech as his little blaster. He didn't even know what the plan was now, but he couldn't let this machine destroy the place that Sonic loved.

Choom-choom-choom-choom-choom!

The cannons rattled off shot after shot directly at the Egg Mech's head. Maybe he'd gotten lucky!

Krang!

With a wave of its arm, the Giant Eggman Robot sliced straight through the Tornado's other wing. Tails had to abandon the plane, jumping just in time to see it in a fireball on a hill outside town. Robotnik's Emerald-amplified monstrosity marched on toward doom and destruction. Tails had brought them all this way. But if Sonic . . . heck, even if Knuckles didn't make it, then what chance did they have?

CHAPTER 18

From his position flying through the air, Sonic could see that the solution to the Giant Eggman Robot was the same as his attack on the labyrinth. He'd have to run right at it.

Luckily, the makeshift missile Robotnik had tagged him with was slow enough to straddle like a cowboy at a rodeo. Sonic was currently bringing the crude projectile around right toward the mech's face.

But first, it was time for Knuckles' shot.

"Robotnik! Face me, you coward!" he called from the street below. Sonic had a glimpse of his strange new ally's showdown from on high, and it did not look good. The echidna pulled his fists up in fighting position. And then with the loud shift of metal joints, the Giant Eggman Robot with the madman's brain struck a kung fu pose in response.

"You deceived me!" Knuckles called from the street.

"Deception is my middle name!" called the cold metal tone of Robotnik from the head in the sky above. "Ha! Another lie. My middle name's actually Gerald. Time to FIGHT!"

Impossibly, a fistfight broke out between the one-hundred-foot mech and the four-foot echidna. Knuckles swung a hard, gnarled fist at the machine, making a tiny scratch in the side of the Giant Eggman Robot's arm.

"Aww, how adorable!" cackled Robotnik's voice.

Whump!

With a long swing of his metal boot, the Giant Eggman Robot punted Knuckles' body off the street and several blocks away. He landed in the middle of the Green Hills High football field as a giant puff of dirt burst into the sky.

"And it's goooooood!" cried the robot with both arms straight in the air.

It was now or never. Sonic stood up, stomped to the back of the missile, and shot them both straight at the Egg Mech.

"Return to sender, Ro-Butt-Nik!" he cried, and jumped off at the last moment. Sonic spun into a ball of crackling blue light and skidded to a halt on the street. In a heartbeat—*Sha-Boom!*—the missile struck the bot's left leg and blew it to pieces.

"Yes!" Sonic called as the mech tumbled. "Who wants an omelet? Because I am cracking eggs!"

But with a set of screeching metal tendrils, the leg reattached itself before the body even hit the dirt. Sonic hadn't stopped the doctor. He'd barely slowed him down. The Master Emerald really would let Robotnik do anything. So what could one kid—no matter how fast—do against it?

Once reassembled, the Giant Eggman Robot shot out a wave of drones to terrorize the streets of Green Hills. It was a nightmare.

"Sonic!" called a voice from Main Street. It was Tom. He stood with Maddie, a wall of shocked soldiers, and a dozen of Sonic's friends.

"Tom! We've got to get everyone out of here!" he yelled, coming to his feet.

"We'll get everyone to safety while you finish Robotnik," Maddie said.

"I . . . I don't think I can," Sonic stammered. "He's too powerful. You were right, Tom. I can't do this alone . . ."

"You're not alone, Sonic." Donut Lord smiled.

"He's with us!" called two voices from down a dark alley. And Tails and Knuckles stepped into the light.

"I knew you'd be back," Sonic said with pride.

"I know, right?" Tails smiled.

"Ready to go for round two?" the hedgehog asked his newest ally.

Knuckles stroked his chin. "I barely felt the last one."

Tom stood up on the back of a truck and called out to those gathered in Green Hills. "You heard Sonic, everyone. We gotta clear the area!"

"Don't worry, guys!" Sonic called to the townspeople and agents alike. "We've got an airtight plan!" He spun and sped his two friends into an alley, panicked. "I lied. I got nothing. Tails, any ideas?"

"If only he had a weak spot." Tails slapped a fist into his palm.

"I suggest the groin," said Knuckles.

"No. What?! No." Sonic stared down the echidna.

"Traditionally, yes, the groin is—"

"Stop saying 'groin'!" He spied out on the street and saw the Giant Eggman Robot scanning for them.

"Hedgehoooog? Where are you?" sang

the empty sound of Robotnik's voice. "Show yourself and meet your dooOOOOoom!"

"I know what his weak spot is," Sonic realized. "*Me.*"

"Come again now?" asked Tails.

"I'm the groin!" Sonic laughed. "Why did Robotnik come back to Green Hills? He's trying to hurt my friends. He wants to destroy my home. I live rent-free in this dude's head! So if I go out there and rile him up . . ."

Knuckles smiled in realization. "Then he'll focus his attack on only you. And that leaves him open for a flanking maneuver from me and the fox."

"Are you sure about this, Sonic?" said Tails, checking one of his endless supply of gizmos. "It's gonna be dangerous."

"With this squad? It's a piece of cake."

Sonic leaned into a stretch before his most

crucial run ever. "What I need you to do is back me up the same way you did in the dance-off. You get me?" The fox nodded eagerly.

"Hedgehog, you are a noble and brave warrior," said Knuckles. "Go to your certain death with honor."

"We're gonna have to work on your pep talks, pal," Sonic said, and set his hands on the ground in a sprinter's stance. "Now let's go!" And with a flick of his feet, he was speeding toward the heart of the town.

"Oh, Eggmaaaaaaaan!" Sonic called as he turned into a bright blue blur one more time and tore a path through the Giant Eggman Robot's legs. But this time, he wasn't alone. To his right, a bright red firecracker of energy tore chunks out of the street as it charged. Over his left shoulder, an orange spark flicked in and out of the air, bursting Robotnik's remaining drones as it went. Knuckles and Tails would keep up their end of the plan. Now Sonic had to do his.

"All right, Mustache! You want me? Come and get me!" Sonic shouted, and beat a path out of town.

"I'm going to squash you like a bug!" Robotnik cried through the mech's mouth.

The Giant Eggman Robot shifted and stomped after him. Sonic had the Eggman right where he wanted him!

"Oh, you're so close!" the hedgehog taunted over his shoulder. "Maybe you need a few days to practice your bug squashing and then come back?"

The Giant Eggman Robot tore into the forest hills outside town. Sonic stopped high up a hill. "What's your big plan here,

Eggman?" he called. "You gonna build a big robot house? Get yourself a big robot wife?"

"I'm going to enslave humanity!" Robotnik's voice was beyond insanity now. "And what are *they* going to do about it? I'll tell you! They'll do exactly as they're told!"

The mech finally zeroed in on Sonic's location, and Robotnik turned over his last surprise card. Laser eyes! The green energy of the Master Emerald poured out of the Giant Eggman Robot's visor.

The ray sliced through the trees, and on the ground, Sonic appeared to be down and out, splayed out on his back, barely breathing.

"Giving up already? Why don't you get up, you pathetic little wretch!" the Giant Eggman Robot called as it stomped toward the broken hedgehog. "Did you not realize you can't beat me? I'm all-powerful . . . all-knowing . . . all-seeing!"

And with a final step of his monster boot, Robotnik came down on Sonic's body with a crushing blow.

CHAPTER 19

Tails struggled to keep Knuckles aloft as they flew out of Green Hills and into the forest lands where the Giant Eggman Robot chased after Sonic. It didn't help that he was holding the bulky echidna by one hand, but he needed the other free in order to work his device.

"Faster, fox! We're losing them!" Knuckles shouted.

"Yeah, but you're really . . . heavy . . ." He

strained and hit a few more keystrokes on his data pad. "Still, we're almost there!"

They zoomed up behind the giant robot and made their ascent to the top of the mech's head while Sonic insulted and outmaneuvered the giant into the tree cover below. Tails fiddled with the knobs on his device.

They got into place. Robotnik's screeching voice reached a crescendo as he cried out, "Did you not realize you can't beat me? I'm all-powerful . . . all-knowing . . . all-seeing!"

Tails couldn't help but close his eyes at the upsetting sight of Robotnik's boot pinning his hero down, but he couldn't stop. The time to act was now!

"Hey, Robotnik!" Knuckles shouted, and punched the Giant Eggman Robot upside its head as hard as he could. The doctor's moment of triumph was delayed as he reached for the pair of interlopers, but Tails led the jump off the robot and into the air.

As they fell, Robotnik swiped around him like a child swatting flies. He brought his big hands together on the red form of his former companion and laughed at the thunderous boom it created.

"Don't mess with me, man! I have a PhD!!" the doctor cheered, only to open his tree-crushing hands and find . . . nothing.

"Missed me!" Knuckles called, running up a metal arm.

"And me, too!" Tails spun through the air in front of the mech's face.

"Now that you mention it," called the voice of Sonic . . . and at that instant, Robotnik flew into an uncontrollable rage.

And it wasn't just those three now. A squadron of Tails buzzed around the robot's head. Half a dozen Knuckles swarmed its legs. And worst of all for Robotnik, a fleet of Sonics zigzagged around the hills ahead, making electric blue crisscrosses as they went. The robot lifted its foot and found no body underneath.

"I! HATE! THAT! HEDGEHOG!" the doctor screamed.

"Maybe you just hate holograms." Knuckles laughed from above the mech's chest plate. "Most of us are them, after all. See? I can lie, too!"

Tails' tech had worked flawlessly. The multiple projections of the trio that he'd programmed on the flight over kept popping up from the device he'd planted on the mech's shoulder—distracting the enraged scientist while Knuckles—the real one—slammed a fist deep into the villain's steel chest cavity and crawled his way into the cockpit. When he finally tore his way into the same space as Robotnik, the echidna didn't hesitate to hit the distracted doctor as hard as he could.

Whomp!

Tails watched as the punch reverberated with waves of green chaos energy.

"The Emerald!" the doctor screamed as he realized the punch had removed the Master Emerald from his body. "No! No! No! No!"

Without the Emerald powering him or his suit, the Giant Eggman Robot started going limp. "Computer! Auxiliary power . . . now!"

The Giant Eggman Robot replied to the command. Even if it was powered by the

Emerald, it was designed by Robotnik and would still obey. The mech jerked back to life, tossing Knuckles aside and digging on the ground for its lost power source.

That's when Tails spotted Sonic. He really had taken a hit for the team. He had been crushed by the Giant Eggman Robot's boot, but he survived and was now crawling toward the shining prize they'd all fought so hard to capture.

"Look out, Sonic!" called a familiar voice. Coming up the road in a pickup were Tom and Maddie, as they tore the vehicle off road.

"Look at the happy little family!" Robotnik sneered, his overconfidence back in full effect. "All the people I hate most in the world in one convenient, smashable place!" The Giant Eggman Robot thrust a fist into the ground, directly between Sonic, the

Wachowskis, and the Emerald itself.

KROOOOOOM!

The ground shook with the force of the blow, but Sonic rose back up and made a beeline for the Emerald. He put his hands on it at last!

But when he opened his hands to inspect the prize, the Emerald shattered into pieces. Its power seemed to go dead.

"What am I supposed to even do with this thing?" Sonic called out.

Robotnik used his mech to set fire to trees in a wide circle around the hedgehog. Tails couldn't reach him. Neither could Knuckles or Tom and Maddie. And he didn't want them to.

"Stand back!" Sonic choked on the smoke as the Emerald fragments fell about his feet. "It's me that he wants!"

Maddie ran through the fire, followed by Tom. "Sonic, we're not going anywhere," they said. "We're your family." The three of them embraced. The Emerald sparkled beneath them just as Robotnik brought down his foot for a final, potentially fatal blow.

WHAM!

Tails watched the only three people on this or any planet who had ever welcomed him get snuffed out just like that. "Noooooooo!" he cried.

"I got him! I finally got him! I always knew I could do it!" Robotnik cheered as he ground his foot deeper into the ground.

Suddenly, light shone out from beneath the Egg Mech's foot, brighter and purer than the Master Emerald's beacon. Tails had to shield his eyes from its powerful golden glow as something lifted the leg of the mech off the ground. With a final push, the foot was cast aside, and everyone could see . . . Sonic?

His fur had transformed into a glowing, golden hue. His quills were longer and pulsated with energy. And as this Sonic rose into the air, Tails could see Tom and Maddie safely behind him, unharmed, staring at him in awe. Tails knew this was something the universe had never seen before. This wasn't just Sonic anymore. This was Super Sonic.

"It's over, Eggman . . . ," Super Sonic called with a voice that shook the trees.

"I like the new look!" Robotnik's voice trembled with fear. "It works for you! Say, let's let bygones be bygones, huh? I did some things. You did some things. Who can even remember how this fight started?!"And then the mad doctor screamed. "At least I can tell you how it ends!" he yelled, and threw a last desperate punch from the Giant Eggman Robot at Super Sonic. The hedgehog flew through the air to dodge the punch. Eggman tried again and again to land a blow, but Super Sonic was like a beam of light shooting across the night sky.

In a flurry of flying blows, Super Sonic wrapped the mech in a web of laser-hot chaos energy. The bot never had a chance. With each new thundering blast, more of its shell fell apart, collapsing finally into a pile of jagged metal rubble. And somewhere within, the weak voice of the all-too-human Robotnik croaked, "I'll . . . get you . . . hedgehog!" But he was down for the count.

Super Sonic landed next to Maddie and Tom. Tails landed next to Knuckles, who kept a fearful distance from their friend.

"Wait! Do not touch him!" Knuckles

called, stopping Tom dead in his tracks. "The hedgehog now holds the power of the Emerald within him. It's too much for any one creature to handle. I'm sorry . . . but he's just not the Sonic you once knew."

Super Sonic floated eerily for a moment, then placed one gloved hand under his armpit.

Braaaaaaaap!

The fart sound hit with the decibels of a bomb blast, and Super Sonic came down laughing hysterically.

"Okay," Knuckles admitted. "He's exactly the Sonic you once knew."

The glowing hedgehog reached his hands into the fur of his chest, and he started to glow as bright as ever before. Sonic lifted his hands to the sky in a blast, the seven Chaos Emeralds shooting from his body. Moving at an ungodly speed, they blasted through space and time itself. Gone forever. And as he floated to the ground, Sonic returned to his natural color.

"Whew!" He wiped the sweat from his brow. "Good to be back in blue. The golden god thing was fun, but this has always been more my color."

"Sonic!" Maddie cried as she and Tom rushed to him for a hug.

"Sonic," Tails said in astonishment. "You were the most powerful hero in the universe just now. Why'd you give it up?"

His hero smiled. "Because I'm not done being a kid yet."

On the edge of the field, Knuckles bent down and looked at the fragments of the initial Master Emerald that lay in the dirt— dark and powerless.

"I've spent my whole life questing for this,"

he said. "Now I have it, and it's worthless."

"You got it all wrong, man," Sonic said, kneeling beside him. "Don't you get it? Centuries ago, our two people went to war with each other over seven Chaos Emeralds. And in their fighting, they brought those Emeralds together to try and hold ultimate power. But it just drove them further apart. I didn't earn the power of the Chaos Emeralds because I was worthier or more powerful than you. I got it because you and I worked together."

Sonic gathered the fragments of the shattered Emerald and squeezed them together in his hands. "Now the seven have returned, and I'll make sure that their chaos is under control from here on out. But you have a mission, too, Knuckles. Take this . . ." With a squeezing of his fists, the green light

shone brightly, and a new Master Emerald
was forged. "Because if the forces of the Chaos
Emeralds ever get out of control again, we'll
need you to use this and restore balance."

Tails beamed at what he was seeing.

"This is just like the legends of old!" he said.
"There were once two orders of heroes who
protected the galaxy from those who would
use the Emeralds for evil . . ."

"But they have all passed to the great
battleground in the sky," Knuckles agreed.

"So we start a new order," Sonic said,
holding his fist out in the air. "The three
of us."

Tails bumped his fist instantaneously. But
Knuckles held back, cautious.

"This is no light task we undertake," the
echidna said. "To use our powers to keep the
universe safe. To watch out for one another—

our new tribe." Finally, he threw his fist in.

"It's called a power bump." Tails smiled. "An Earth custom. An unbreakable promise."

Sonic grinned. "Way past cool," he said.

CHAPTER 20

Things were moving slower than ever before, and Sonic loved it.

The summer days in Green Hills seemed to stretch out forever, and as the townsfolk assembled for an exhibition game at the baseball field, everyone was content to let the innings roll on and on.

Sonic leaned lazily on an elbow in the announcer's box, Ozzy at his feet, as he called the play on the field with a nice, comfortable drawl. "It's a beautiful day for baseball here in Green Hills, folks," he said. "And an exciting lineup, too, with the debut of two new players to your hometown roster."

On the field, Donut Lord and Maddie were spread out between left center and right center, hopefully far back enough to catch any of the bat-breaking hits that were sure to be coming. But that was only if the pitcher didn't deliver a perfect game.

"On the mound is the rookie sensation Miles 'Tails' Prower!" Sonic called as his wingman wound up. "He's a real ace, folks, but look out for who he's facing."

At home plate, Knuckles held a bat over his shoulder with a puzzled look on his face. "I don't understand," the gruff echidna said. "What has this spherical object done to deserve such an attack?"

"It's not an attack!" Sonic called across the field, his hand covering the announcer's mic. "You just want to hit it as hard as you can and then run around the bases!"

"If my goal is to arrive where I am standing, why run at all?"

Tails laughed. "It's a game, man! Try and have a little fun."

"Fun!" Knuckles grunted and lifted the bat into his stance. "Huh."

Tails let fly a solid fastball, but before it was halfway to the plate, Sonic had sped his way into the catcher's position and held his mitt out in case Knuckles whiffed.

Swap!

The pitch landed in Sonic's glove a little too gently for a strike. "Come on, Tails! Give him the heat!" he called, throwing it back.

"Hope you're ready for my real fastball, Knuckles!"

"I was not ready before, but now I shall dishonor you and your so-called 'fastball'!"

From the outfield, the adults called them to order. "It's just a game, guys!" said Maddie as Tom coached. "Remember to keep your elbow up, Knuck! Eye on the ball and just give it a ride!"

"A ride to where?" Knuckles wondered. But he had no time to ponder. The next pitch was thrown. As it sped to the plate, the bat fell to the ground. And then . . .

CRACK!

Knuckles punched the ball straight on, sending it soaring into the air. It rose far over Tom's and Maddie's heads, past the scoreboard, and into the parking lot of a restaurant two blocks east.

"I think that was our last ball," Tom said as they ran in from the field.

"No fair! That shouldn't count!" cried Tails.

"Victory is mine!" Knuckles shouted, and flexed.

It was a good ending for the game. Later, they'd go for ice cream, then stay up late for a movie. And then tomorrow, they'd do it all again. For once, it was a slow pace Sonic could be happy with, because he had his own crew to share the experience.

"I'm happy for you, pal," Tom said as they hung back on the walk to the ice-cream parlor. "You've finally got your perfect wingmen. These guys are the perfect friends to grow up with."

Sonic almost blushed. He still wondered, of course. What other threats would be out there? What shadowy figures wanted to upset the life these three were building? How long before they'd be called to action again?

But for the moment, none of that mattered. All that mattered was that he was here in the place he belonged—and with the people he belonged with. "It's not just the crew that makes me happy," Sonic said. "It's everything we've got here . . . Dad."

Donut Lord threw his arm around Sonic, and they walked toward home.

Left alone on the baseball field is a sports cooler with drinks and ice. Resting in the center of the cooler is the Master Emerald. In an instant, Sonic is next to the cooler. "Ooh! Can't forget this!" And in a blue blur, the cooler disappears.

THE END